Praise for the Work of
LOUIS L'AMOUR

MONUMENT ROCK

"[A] compelling blend of explosive action, period detail, humor, and insights about human nature."
—*USA Today*

END OF THE DRIVE

"Awesome immediacy, biting as creosote slapped on a fencepost."
—*Kirkus Reviews*

BEYOND THE GREAT SNOW MOUNTAINS

"L'Amour's brassy women and dusty men keep the action of these cinematic stories hot. . . . These adventure tales offer their share of the high drama L'Amour is famous for."
—*Publishers Weekly*

OFF THE MANGROVE COAST

"L'Amour was a man who lived life to the fullest. Fortunately for the rest of us, he remembered the details and possessed the talent to bring those experiences to life on paper."
—*Booklist*

Bantam Books by Louis L'Amour

NOVELS

Bendigo Shafter
Borden Chantry
Brionne
The Broken Gun
The Burning Hills
The Californios
Callaghen
Catlow
Chancy
The Cherokee Trail
Comstock Lode
Conagher
Crossfire Trail
Dark Canyon
Down the Long Hills
The Empty Land
Fair Blows the Wind
Fallon
The Ferguson Rifle
The First Fast Draw
Flint
Guns of the Timberlands
Hanging Woman Creek
The Haunted Mesa
Heller with a Gun
The High Graders
High Lonesome
Hondo
How the West Was Won
The Iron Marshal
The Key-Lock Man
Kid Rodelo
Kilkenny
Killoe
Kilrone
Kiowa Trail
Last of the Breed
Last Stand at
  Papago Wells
The Lonesome Gods
The Man Called Noon
The Man from
  Skibbereen
The Man from
  the Broken Hills
Matagorda
Milo Talon
The Mountain
  Valley War
North to the Rails
Over on the Dry Side
Passin' Through
The Proving Trail
The Quick and the Dead
Radigan
Reilly's Luck

The Rider of Lost Creek
Rivers West
The Shadow Riders
Shalako
Showdown at
  Yellow Butte
Silver Canyon
Sitka
Son of a Wanted Man
Taggart
The Tall Stranger
To Tame a Land
Tucker
Under the
  Sweetwater Rim
Utah Blaine
The Walking Drum
Westward the Tide
Where the Long
  Grass Blows

SHORT STORY COLLECTIONS

Beyond the Great
  Snow Mountains
Bowdrie
Bowdrie's Law
Buckskin Run
The Collected Short
  Stories of Louis
  L'Amour (vols. 1–7)
Dutchman's Flat
End of the Drive
From the Listening Hills
The Hills of Homicide
Law of the Desert Born
Long Ride Home
Lonigan
May There Be a Road
Monument Rock
Night Over
  the Solomons
Off the Mangrove Coast
The Outlaws of
  Mesquite
The Rider of
  the Ruby Hills
Riding for the Brand
The Strong Shall Live
The Trail to Crazy Man
Valley of the Sun
War Party
West from Singapore
West of Dodge
With These Hands
Yondering

SACKETT TITLES

Sackett's Land
To the Far
  Blue Mountains
The Warrior's Path
Jubal Sackett
Ride the River
The Daybreakers
Sackett
Lando
Mojave Crossing
Mustang Man
The Lonely Men
Galloway
Treasure Mountain
Lonely on the Mountain
Ride the Dark Trail
The Sackett Brand
The Sky-Liners

THE HOPALONG CASSIDY NOVELS

The Riders of High Rock
The Rustlers
  of West Fork
The Trail to Seven Pines
Trouble Shooter

NONFICTION

Education of a
  Wandering Man
Frontier
The Sackett Companion:
  A Personal Guide to
  the Sackett Novels
A Trail of Memories:
  The Quotations of
  Louis L'Amour,
  compiled by
  Angelique L'Amour

POETRY

Smoke from This Altar

LOST TREASURES

Louis L'Amour's Lost
  Treasures: Volume 1
  (with Beau L'Amour)
No Traveller Returns
  (with Beau L'Amour)
Louis L'Amour's Lost
  Treasures: Volume 2
  (with Beau L'Amour)

READY TO FIGHT

CORBUS STARED AT young Mike Bastian, a cold hint of danger filtering through. "Suppose I don't want to drink with no tenderfoot brat?"

Corbus never saw what happened. His brain warned him as Bastian's left hand moved, but he never saw the right. The left smashed his lips, and the right cracked on the angle of his jaw. He hit the floor on his shoulder blades, out cold.

Fletcher and the third tough hesitated. Corbus was on the floor and Bastian was not smiling. "You boys want a drink or do we go on from here?"

"What if a man drawed a gun instead of usin' his fists?" Fletcher asked.

"I'd kill him," Mike replied.

SON OF A WANTED MAN

A NOVEL

Louis L'Amour

Postscript by Beau L'Amour

BANTAM
NEW YORK

2024 Bantam Books Mass Market Edition

Copyright © 1984 by Louis D. & Katherine E. L'Amour
1983 Trust
Postscript by Beau L'Amour copyright © 2024
by Beau L'Amour

Published in the United States by Bantam Books,
an imprint of Random House, a division of
Penguin Random House LLC, New York.

Bantam & B colophon is a registered trademark of
Penguin Random House LLC.

Originally published in the United States
by Bantam Books, an imprint of Random House, a division
of Penguin Random House LLC, in 1984.

ISBN 978-0-593-72521-4
Ebook ISBN 978-0-593-72522-1

Map: Alan McKnight
Cover art: Louis Glanzman
Photograph of Louis L'Amour:
John Hamilton—Globe Photos, Inc.

Printed in the United States of America

randomhousebooks.com

Book design by Edwin A. Vazquez

2 4 6 8 9 7 5 3 1

Bantam Books mass market edition: October 2024

To Badie-Guy
My Ponca Friend . . .

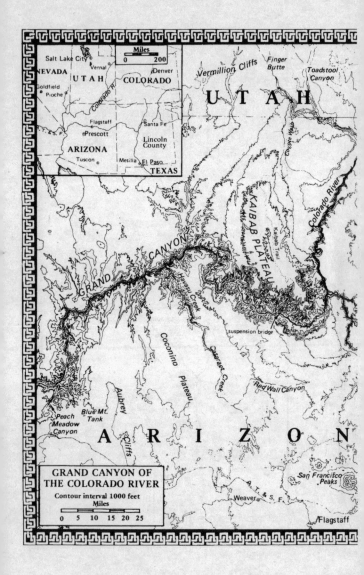

GRAND CANYON OF
THE COLORADO RIVER

Contour interval 1000 feet
Miles

0   5   10   15   20   25

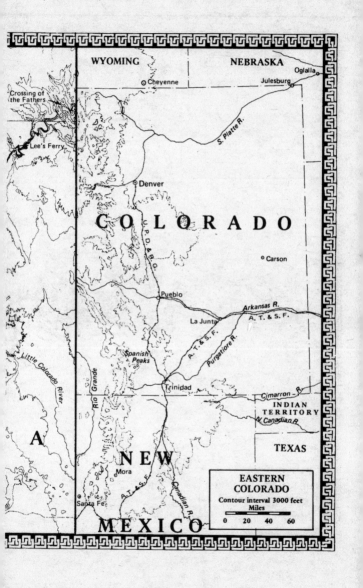

AUTHOR'S NOTE

To DEFEND AGAINST the kind of outlaws I write about in *Son of a Wanted Man*, and as the towns of the western frontier began to develop and become more populated, there was a great need for law enforcement officials to become more professional in their approach to dealing with lawbreakers. Dave Cook, whom I mention in this novel, was a real marshal who began to organize the individual marshals of towns in the West in an effort to get them to cooperate in tracking down criminals and bringing them to justice.

There are two town marshals who play important roles in this story and who support the ideas of Dave Cook, and they will both be old friends to my readers: Borden Chantry and Tyrel Sackett. Tyrell Sackett, of course, appears in a number of the novels I have written over the years about the Sackett family. I know from the mail I get that the "Mora gunfighter" is a particular favorite of many readers so I am glad to have been able to work him into this book. Tyrel has met up once before with Chantry in the novel *Borden Chantry*, where Chantry solved the murder of Joe Sackett, Tyrel's brother.

SON OF A WANTED MAN

CHAPTER 1

THE WINTER SNOWS were melting in the forests of the Kaibab, and the red-orange Vermilion Cliffs were streaked with melting frost. Deer were feeding in the forest glades among the stands of ponderosa and fir, and trout were leaping in the sun-sparkled streams. A shadow moved under the ponderosa, then was gone.

Five deer fed on the grass along the bank of a mountain stream back of Finger Butte, their coats mottled with the light and shadow of sunlight through the leaves.

It was very still. Water rippled around the roots of a tree where the soil had washed away, and gurgled cheerfully among the rocks. A buck's tail twitched, twitched again, and the regal head lifted, turning its nostrils to the wind, reading it cautiously, but the reading was betrayal, for the shadow under the pines was downwind of him.

A faint breeze sifted through the grass and stirred the leaves, and with the breeze the shadow moved into the sunlight and became a man, standing motionless not twenty feet from the nearest deer.

Straight and tall he stood in gray buckskins. He wore no hat, and his hair long. Lean and brown, his black hair loose, he waited until the buck's head lifted again, looking right at him.

A startled snort and the buck sprang away. The others followed. Mike Bastian stood with his hands on his hips, watching them go.

Another man came through the trees behind him, a lean, wiry old man with a gray mustache and blue eyes alive with humor.

"What do you think of that, Roundy?" Bastian asked. "Could your Apache beat that? Another step and I could have touched him."

Roundy spat into the grass. "No Apache I ever knowed could do better, son. An' I never seen the day I could do as well. You're good, Mike, really good. I am surely glad you're not huntin' my hair!" He drew his pipe from his pocket and began stoking it. "We're headin' back for Toadstool Canyon, Mike. Your pa sent for us."

"No trouble, is there?"

"None I know of, although things don't look good. They don't look good at all. No, I think your pa figures it's time you rode out with the bunch."

Mike Bastian squatted on his heels, glancing around the glade. This was what he liked, and he did not want to leave. Nor did he like what he was going back to face. "I believe you're right, Roundy. Pa said I was to ride out in the spring when the boys went, and it is about time."

He tugged a blade of grass and chewed on it. "I wonder where they will go this time?"

"Whatever it is, and wherever it is, it will be well planned. Your pa would have made a fine general, boy. He's got the head for it. He never forgets a thing."

"You've been with him a long time, haven't you?"

"Mighty long. I was with him before he found you. I met him in Mexico during the War, longer ago than I care to remember. I was just a youngster then, myself."

From the grass he took up a fallen pine cone. "Son! *Look!*" He tossed the pine cone into the air.

Mike Bastian palmed his gun and it belched flame, then again. The second shot spattered the pine cone into flying brown chips.

"Not bad," Roundy said, "but you shot too quick. You've got to get over that, Mike. Most times one shot is all you'll get."

Side by side they started back through the woods. The earth was spongy with a thick bed of pine needles. An occasional break in the trees offered a glimpse of the far-off San Francisco peaks, with clouds shrouding their summits. Roundy was not as tall as the younger man, but he walked with the long, easy stride of the woodsman. Coming to a break in the forest that permitted them a long view of the wild, broken canyon country to the east, Roundy spoke. "Your pa picked mighty well. Nobody in God's world could find him in all that."

"There's Indians," Bastian reminded, "and some of the Mormons know that country."

"He doesn't bother them and they don't bother

him," Roundy said. "That's why his outfit needs a tight rein."

They walked on, in silence. Several times Bastian paused to study the ground, reading the tracks to see who or what had passed since they had passed. "This here is somethin' you better not do again," Roundy suggested, "comin' back the way we went out. Somebody could be layin' for us."

"Who?"

"Ah, now. That's the question. Nobody is supposed to know your pa's plans for you, but there's always the chance somebody might. Believe me, son, nothin' is a secret for long, an' you can just bet some of the boys have been doin' some thinkin' about you."

They paused again, studying the country around, and Roundy put the question that had been bothering him for months. "Mike? If Ben's ready for you to go out, what will you do?"

"Go, I guess. What choice do I have?"

"You're sure? You're sure you want to be an outlaw?"

"Wasn't that why he raised me? To take over from him?" There was an edge of bitterness in Mike's tone. "Wasn't I to take over when Ben Curry stepped aside?"

"That's what you were raised for, all right." Roundy poked at the pine needles with his toe. "But it's your life you have to live. Ben Curry can't live it for you, and you can't live his life for him, no matter how much he wants it.

"The thing to remember, Mike, is that things have

changed since Ben an' me rode into this country to-gether. It's no longer wild and free like it was. Folks are movin' in, settlin' the country, buildin' homes.

"Getaways won't be so easy no more, and the kind of men you ride with will change. Fact is, they have already changed.

"When Ben an' me rode into this country it was wide open. Most banks had been mighty hard on a poor man, ready to foreclose at the slightest chance, and the railroads gave all the breaks to the big cattle shippers, so nobody cared too much if a train was robbed or a bank. If you killed somebody, especially a man with a wife and kids—well, that was some-thing else. If you just robbed a bank or train the pos-ses would chase you more for fun than actually to catch you. It was a break in the work they were doin'. They'd get out, run an outlaw for a while but not too serious about it.

"Kill a man? That was different. They'd chase you for keeps then, and they'd catch you. That's why Ben Curry wouldn't stand for killin', an' he's been known to personally kill a man who disobeyed that order."

"He actually did?"

"Seen it myself. It was Dan Peeples, and Dan was a high hand with a gun. They'd robbed a bank in Wyoming an' as they were ridin' out of town this young feller came out of an alley, blundered right in the way, and Dan Peeples shot him.

"Folks seen it. Folks knew it was deliberate. Well, we rode on three, four miles an' Ben pulled up. He turned to Dan Peeples an' he said, 'I said no killin', Dan.'

"Dan, he just grinned an' said, 'Well, he got in the way. Anyway, what's one farm kid, more or less?'

"Ben Curry said, 'When I say no killin', I mean it.'

"Dan, he says, 'So?' And Ben shot him. Dan saw it comin' and reached but he was too slow, so Ben left him layin' there for the posse to find."

"What if they got cornered?"

"That was different. If they had to fight their way out, well an' good, an' a time or two that happened. Your pa was against needless killin', an' the word got around. The outlaws knew it, but the townsfolk, ranchers, an' lawmen knew it, too."

"I've heard some of the stories."

"No way you could miss. Ben Curry's kind breed stories. In them old days many a man rustled a few head to get started, and sometimes a broke cowhand would stand up a stage and nobody took it too serious, but it isn't like that anymore. The country is growin' up and changing viewpoints. More than that, it is Ben himself."

"You think he's too big?"

"What else? Your pa controls more country than there is in New York State! Right under his thumb! And he's feared over much of the west by those who really know about him, but not many do.

"Outside of his own crowd nobody has seen Ben Curry in years, at least, not to know who he was. Mighty few know his power, although there's a rumor around that somewhere there lives a man who rides herd on more than a hundred outlaws. Much of his success lies in the fact that nobody believes it.

"His men ride out and meet at a given point. They

ride alone or in pairs, never more than three together at a time until the job is pulled, then they break up an' scatter.

"He plans ever' job himself, with maybe one or two settin' in. He's scouted or had the job scouted by somebody he can trust. It is planned, rehearsed, then done.

"Mostly folks lay the robberies to driftin' cowhands, to Jesse James or somebody else. He pulls jobs anywhere from Canada to Mexico, and from San Antone to Los Angeles."

Roundy started off along the trail. "He's been the brains, all right, but don't ever forget it was those guns of his kept things in line. Lately, he hasn't had to use his guns. Kerb Perrin, Rigger Molina, or somebody else will handle discipline. He's become too big, Ben Curry has. He's like a king, and the king isn't gettin' any younger."

He stopped in the trail and turned around. "How d'you suppose Perrin will take it when he hears about you takin' over? You think he'll stand still for that?"

"I doubt if he will," Mike said thoughtfully. "I imagine he's done some planning on his own."

"You can bet he has! So has Molina, and neither one of them will stop at murder to get what they want. Your pa still has them buffaloed, I think, but that won't matter when the showdown comes. And I figure the time has come."

"Now?" Mike was incredulous.

"Mike, I never told you, and I know Ben hasn't, but Ben has a family."

"A *family*?" Mike Bastian was shocked. "But I—!"

"He has a wife and two daughters, and they have no idea he's an outlaw. Wouldn't believe it if you told 'em. Their home is down near Tucson someplace, but occasionally they come to a ranch he owns in Red Wall Canyon, a ranch supposedly owned by Voyle Ragan. Ben visits them there."

"Who else knows this?"

"Nary a soul, and don't you be tellin' anyone. Ben, he always wanted a son, and never had one, so when your real pa was killed down at Mesilla, Ben took you to raise. That was nigh onto eighteen years ago, and since then he's spent a lot of time an' thought on you. A long time later he told me he was going to raise you to take over whatever he left."

"What about my real father? My family?"

Roundy shrugged. "I never did get the straight of that, and there may be other stories. The way I heard, it was your real pa was killed by 'Paches whilst you was off in the brush somewhere. They come down, killed your pa, stole your horses, and looted the wagon. They were bein' chased by soldiers out of El Paso or somewhere an' it was a sort of hit-an'-run thing. The soldiers brought you back to town an' Ben took you to raise."

"Kind of him."

"Yes, it was. Not many men would do such a thing, them days. Most of them just didn't want the responsibility or wouldn't take the time. For several years it was just you an' him, an' he tried to teach you everything he knew.

"Look at it. You can track like an Apache. In the woods you're a ghost, and I doubt if old Ben Curry himself can throw a gun as fast and accurate as you. You can ride anything that wears hair, an' what you don't know about cards, dice, roulette, and all the rest of it, nobody knows. You can handle a knife, fight with your fists, and open anything made in the way of safes and locks.

"Along with that he's seen you got a good education, so's you can handle yourself in any kind of company. I doubt if any boy ever got the education and training you've had, and now Ben is ready to step back an' let you take over."

"So he can join his wife and daughters?"

"Uh-huh. He just wants to step out of the picture, go somewhere far off, and live a quiet life. He's gettin' no younger and he wants to take it easy in his last years. You see, Mike, Ben's been afraid of only one thing. That's poverty. He had a lot of it as a youngster. I reckon that was one reason he taken you to raise, he knowed what you were up against, if you lived at all.

"Now he's made his pile, but he knows he can't get out alive unless he has somebody younger, stronger, and smarter to take control of what he's built. That's where you come in."

"Why not let Perrin have it?"

"You know the answer to that. Perrin is mean and he's dangerous. He'd have gone off the deep end long ago if it hadn't been for Ben Curry. He's a good second man but a damn poor leader. That goes for Molina, too. He'd have killed fifty times if he hadn't known that Ben would kill him when he got back.

"No, neither could handle it, and the whole shootin' match would go to pieces in sixty days left to either of them. More than that, a lot of people would get killed, inside an' outside the gang."

Little of what Roundy was saying was new to Bastian, yet he was curious as to why the old man was saying it. The two had been together a lot and knew each other as few men ever did. They had gone through storm, hunger, and thirst together, living in the desert and mountains, returning only occasionally to the rendezvous in Toadstool Canyon.

Obviously there was purpose in Roundy's bringing up the subject, and Bastian waited, listening. Over the years he had learned that Roundy rarely talked at random. He spoke when he had something to say, something important. Yet even as they talked he was aware of all that was about him. A quail had moved into the tall grass near the stream, and ahead of them a squirrel moved in the crotch of a tree, and only minutes ago a gray wolf had crossed the path where they walked.

Roundy had said he was a woodsman, and it was true that he felt more at home in the woods and wild country than anywhere else. The idea of taking over the leadership of the outlaws filled him with unease. Always he had been aware that this time would come, and he had been schooled for it, but until now it had always been pleasantly remote. Now, suddenly, it was at hand.

Was he afraid of responsibility? Or was he simply

afraid? Searching his thoughts he could find no fear. As for responsibility, he had been so prepared and conditioned for his role that it was a natural step.

He thought of Kerb Perrin and Rigger Molina. Was he afraid? No, he was not. Both men had been tolerant and even friendly when he was a boy, Molina especially. Yet as he grew older and became a man they had withdrawn. Did they realize the role that he was being prepared for?

They knew him, but how much did they know? None of them had seen him shoot, for example. At least, none that he knew.

Roundy interrupted his thoughts by stopping to study the country ahead. "Mike," Roundy said, "the country is growing up. Last year some of our raids raised merry hell, and the boys had a hard time getting away. Folks don't like having their lives disrupted, and when the boys ride out this year they will be riding into trouble.

"Folks don't look at an outlaw as they used to. He isn't regarded as some wild youngster full of liquor and excess energy. He's a bad man, dangerous to the community, and he's stealing money folks have saved.

"Now they see an outlaw like a wolf, and every man will be hunting him. Before you go into this you'd better think it over, and think seriously.

"You know Ben Curry, and I know you like him, as well you should. He did a lot for you. At the same time, Ben had no right to raise you to be an outlaw. He chose his own way, of his own free will, but you should be free to do the same.

"No man has a right to say to another, 'This you

must be.' Nobody ever asked you did you want to be an outlaw, although as a youngster you might have said yes. Looked at from afar it seems romantic an' excitin'. Well, take it from me, it ain't. It's hard, dirty, and rough. It's hangin' out with mean, bitter people; it's knowin' cheap, tricky women who are just like the outlaws, out to make a fast buck the easiest way they can."

The old man stopped to relight his pipe, and Mike kept silent, waiting for Roundy to continue. "I figure ever' man has a right to choose his own way, and no matter what Ben's done for you, you got that right.

"I don't know what you'll do, but if you decide to step out of the gang I don't want to be around when it happens. Old Ben will be fit to be tied. I don't figure he's ever really thought about how you feel. He's only figuring on gettin' out and havin' somebody to take over.

"He's built somethin' here, and in his way he's proud of it. Ben would have been a builder and an organizer in whatever direction he chose, but he's not thinkin' straight. Moreover, Ben hasn't been on a raid for years. He doesn't know how it is anymore.

"Oh, he plans! He studies the layout of the towns, the banks, and the railroads, but he doesn't see how folks are changin'. He doesn't listen to them talk. It isn't just saloons, corrals, honky-tonks, and gamblin' anymore. Folks have churches an' schools. They don't want lead flyin' whilst their kids are walkin' to school.

"Right now you're an honest man. You're clear as a whistle. Once you become an outlaw a lot will change. You will have to kill, don't forget that. It is one thing to kill in defense of your home, your family, or your country. It is quite another thing when you kill for money or for power."

"Do you think I'll have to kill Perrin an' Molina?"

"Unless they kill you first. You're good with a gun, Mike. Aside from Ben Curry you're the best I ever saw, but shootin' at a target isn't like shootin' at a man who's shootin' back at you.

"Take Billy the Kid, this Lincoln County gunman we've been hearin' about. Frank an' George Coe, Dick Brewer, Jesse Evans, any one of them can probably shoot as good as Ben. The difference is that part down inside where the nerves should be. Well, that was left out. When he starts shootin' or they shoot at him, he's like ice.

"Kerb Perrin is that way, too. He's cold, and steady as a rock. Rigger Molina's another kind of cat. He explodes all over the place. He's white-hot but deadly as a rattler.

"Five men cornered Molina one time out of Julesburg. When the shootin' was over four of them were down and the fifth was holdin' a gunshot arm. Molina, he rode out under his own power. He's a shaggy wolf, that one! Wild, uncurried, an' big as a bear!"

Roundy paused, puffing on his pipe. "Sooner or later, Mike, there'll be a showdown. It will be one or the other, maybe both of them, and God help you!"

CHAPTER 2

LISTENING TO ROUNDY, Mike remembered that time and time again Ben Curry had warned him to confide in no one. Betrayal could come from anyone, at any time, for even the best of people liked to talk and to repeat what they knew. And there were always those who might take a drink too many or who might talk to get themselves off a hook. What nobody knew, nobody could tell.

Obviously, Ben practiced what he preached, for until now Mike had not even guessed Ben might have a life other than the one he lived in and about Toadstool Canyon. Of course, he did ride off alone from time to time, but he was understood to be scouting jobs or tapping his own sources of information.

Nobody knew what the next job was to be, or where, until Ben Curry called a conference around the big table in his stone house. At such times the table would be covered with maps and diagrams. The location of the town in relation to the country around, the possible approaches to and routes away from town, the layout of the bank itself or whatever was to be robbed, and information on the people employed there and their probable reaction to a robbery.

The name of the town was never on the map. If it was recognized by anyone present he was advised to keep his mouth shut until told.

Distances had been measured and escape routes chosen, with possible alternatives in the event of trouble. Fresh horses awaited them and first-aid treatment if required. Each job was planned months in advance and a final check made to see that nothing unexpected had come up just before the job was pulled.

There were ranches and hideouts located at various places to be used only in case of need, and none were known criminal resorts. Each location was given only at the time of the holdup, and rarely would a location be used again.

Far more than Roundy imagined had Mike Bastian been involved in the planning of past ventures. For several years he had been permitted to take part in the original planning to become acquainted with Ben Curry's methods of operation.

"Some day," Ben Curry warned, "you will ride out with the boys, and you must be ready. I do not plan for you to ride out often. Just a time or two to get the feel of it and to prove yourself to the others. When you do go you will have charge of the job, and when you return you will make the split."

"Will they stand for that?"

"They'd damn' well better! I'll tell 'em, but you'll be your own enforcer—and no shootin'. You run this outfit without that, or you ain't the man I think you are."

Looking back, he could see how carefully Ben Curry had trained him, teaching him little by little and watching how he received it. Deliberately, Ben had kept him from any familiarity with the outlaws he would lead. Only Roundy, who was no outlaw at all, knew him well. Roundy, an old mountain man, had taught him Indian lore and the ways of the mountains. Both of them had showed him trails known to no others. Several times outlaws had tried to pump him for information, but he had professed to know nothing.

The point Roundy now raised worried him. The Ben Curry he knew was a big, gruff, kindly man, even if grim and forbidding at times. He had taken in the homeless boy, giving him kindness and care, raising him as a son. For all of that Mike Bastian had no idea that Ben had a wife and family, or any other life than this. Ben had planned and acted with care and shrewdness.

"You ain't done nothin' wrong," Roundy suggested. "The law doesn't know you or want you. You're clean. Whatever you knew about those maps an' such, that was just a game your pa played with you."

And that was how it had been for the first few years. It was not until recently that he had begun to realize those maps and diagrams were deadly serious, and it was then he had begun to worry.

"Nobody knows Ben Curry," Roundy said. "Any

warrants there may have been forgotten. He ain't ridden out on a job in fifteen year. When he decides to quit he'll simply disappear and appear somewheres else under another name and with his family. He'll be a retired gentleman who made his pile out West."

Roundy paused. "He'll be wanted nowhere, he'll be free to live out his years, and he'll have you trained to continue what he started."

"Suppose I don't want to?"

Roundy looked up at him, his wise old eyes measuring and shrewd. "Then you'll have to tell him," he said. "You will have to face him with it."

Mike Bastian felt a chill. Face that old man? He shook his head. "I don't know," he said, "if I could."

"Is it you don't want to hurt him? Or are you simply scared?"

Mike shrugged. "A little of both, I guess. But then, why shouldn't I take over? It's an exciting life."

"It is that," Roundy commented dryly. "You got no idea how excitin' until you tell Kerb Perrin and Rig Molina who's boss."

Mike laughed. "I can see them," he said. The smile faded. "Has Ben Curry thought of that?"

"You bet he has! Why's he had you workin' with a six-gun all these years?"

Here, around the Vermilion Cliffs was the only world he knew. This was his country, but what lay outside? He could only guess.

Could he make it out there? He could become a gambler. He knew cards, dice, faro, roulette, all of it. Or he could punch cows, he supposed. Somewhere out beyond this wilderness of rust-red cliffs there was another world where men lived honest, hardworking lives, where they worked all day and went home at night to a wife, children, and a fireside. It was a world from which he had been taken, a world in which his father had lived, and his mother, he supposed, although he knew nothing of her.

"Roundy? What do you know about who my parents were?"

The old man stared at the ground. He had known the question would be asked someday. He had wondered how he would answer it. Now, faced with it at last, he hedged.

"You were in Mesilla when he found you. The way I heard it, your pa was killed by 'Paches. I reckon your ma was dead before that, or why else wouldn't she be with you, young as you were?"

"I've wondered about that," Mike said quietly. "I suppose she had died before." He paused. "I guess a man is always curious. Pa, I mean Ben, he never speaks of it."

They had reached their horses, grazing on a meadow among the aspen. Roundy spoke. "You'd better be thinkin' of the future, not the past. You'd best be thinkin' of what you're goin' to tell Ben when he tells you you're ridin' out with the boys."

Roundy stared after Mike as he walked toward the horses. He had never had a son, none that he knew of, anyway. Yet for years he had worked with Mike Bastian, leading him, training him, talking to him. He had spent more time with him than most fathers did with their sons, and not only because it was his job.

Now he was scared. He admitted it, he was scared. He was scared for more reasons than one, because Ben Curry had made a mistake.

Roundy only heard of it after the fact. Usually he sat in on the planning, keeping well back in a corner and rarely putting in a comment, but in this case he had been out in the hills with Mike and had not heard until later.

When they were alone, he faced Ben with it. "Mora? You've got to be crazy!"

Ben Curry pulled up in his walking across the room. "What's that? Why?"

Roundy had never spoken to him like that, and Ben was startled. He stared at the old man. "What's wrong?" he asked.

"You said Mora. You sent the boys into Mora. That's Tyrel Sackett's town."

"Who?"

"Ben, you've been back in the hills too long. You don't listen anymore. Tyrel Sackett is that gunfighter who was in the land-grant fight. He's hell on wheels."

"I never heard of him. Anyway," he added, "he was in Santa Fe. I made sure of that."

"And when he comes home?"

"The boys will be long gone and far away."

"Ben, you don't know him. He won't stand for it, Ben. He'll never quit until he knows who, how, and why. I know him."

Ben shrugged. "Too late now. Anyway, there's no

tracks. Rain washed everything out, and the boys never even raised a whisper. Sixty thousand on that one. Most of the town's savings in one swoop."

Roundy said no more, but in the weeks that followed he grew increasingly worried. Mike would be going out soon, and the country was tightening up. That was bad enough without incurring the anger of a man like Tyrel Sackett, a man who was a master at tracking and trailing.

A few months later, Ben had commented on it. "What did I tell you? Nothing came of that Mora business."

Roundy, squatted on his heels at the fireplace, nursing a cup of coffee, had glanced up. "It hasn't been a year yet. You can bet Sackett hasn't forgotten."

APPROXIMATELY FOUR HUNDRED miles to the east a train was stopping even as he spoke, stopping at a small, sandblasted town in eastern Colorado, a town with only a freight car for a depot.

One man stepped down from the train, a tall young man in a black suit. He stood there, watching the train pull away.

Glancing out the window, Borden Chantry had seen the train slow, then come to a stop, and as it rarely stopped, he waited, watching.

He had been doing his accounts, never a job he liked, but the taxpayers demanded to know where every dollar went, and as town marshal he had to account for every fine, every cent spent feeding those in jail.

He saw the lone man swing down, and he got up. "Ma?" He spoke to his wife, Bess. "Set another place. We're goin' to have comp'ny. Tyrel Sackett just got off the train."

CHAPTER 3

WHEN THE DISHES were put away and the table wiped clean, Borden Chantry refilled their coffee cups. He swung a chair around with its back to the table and straddled it, leaning his thick forearms on the back.

"This is a long way from Mora," he suggested.

"Things are quiet over there, and I've got a good deputy. Thought I'd ride the cars over and have a little talk."

Borden sipped his coffee, and waited.

"Ever hear of Dave Cook?"

"Officer up Denver way, ain't he?" Borden paused. "My wife says I shouldn't say 'ain't' but I keep forgettin'."

"That's right. Denver. He's got an idea of organizing all the officers so we all work together. You know how it's been—you keep the peace in your town and I in mine. If somebody kills a man here, why should I care if he keeps out of trouble in Mora? Well, Dave thinks we should all work together."

"I'm for it."

"About a year ago we had a holdup in Mora.

Store holdup, but a store that banked money for folks. Had quite a lot of money, sixty thousand dollars, in the store safe. I was out of town," he added.

"Handy," Chantry commented.

"I thought so. Just too handy. Sixty thousand in the safe and the sheriff out of town. Makes for easy pickin's, 'specially when the note that got me down to Santa Fe was a fake."

"Forged?"

"No, and that's another interesting part. It was a note from my brother Orrin and it simply said, *Need you.* When a Sackett gets that kind of word he just naturally comes a-running. The trouble was that note was one Orrin wrote to his former wife a couple of years ago.

"Now the question is, how did somebody get hold of that note and where's it been all that time?

"Orrin wrote that note. He remembered it well because it was a troublesome time, but he never saw it again." Tyrel paused. "Seems to me somebody was mighty farsighted. They come on that note somehow, some way, and they just kept it against a needful time."

"It doesn't seem reasonable. How would anybody know they might need such a note years in advance?"

"Think of it, Bord. That note doesn't explain anything and there's no date, so somebody saw it might be useful and filed it away, and that somebody had to be a crook."

"They robbed your bank."

"Exactly. That says that somebody two years ago

thought that note might be useful, somebody who was probably a thief at the time."

Sackett put down his cup. "Let me lay it out for you. At noontime folks are home eating. The streets are empty, only one man in the store, and then of a sudden there are three other men. The storekeeper was bound and gagged, money taken from the safe, as it was rarely locked in the daytime, and the shade drawn on the front door window. The three men leave by the back door.

"Nigh onto two hours later a fellow comes to the store, finds it locked, and goes away. Sometime later another comes, only he don't go away but walks around to the back door. He's out of tobacco and he'll be damned if he's goin' to go without.

"The back door is closed. He knocks and it opens under his fist and he hears thumpin' inside. He goes in and finds the teller all tied up an' the money gone."

"Any descriptions?"

"Three youngish, middle-sized men, one of them wearin' a polka-dot shirt. The teller says they moved fast, knew right where the money was, and weren't in the store more than five minutes, probably not more than three. Nobody said a word amongst them, just to the teller to keep his mouth shut if he wanted to live."

"Nobody saw them comin' or goin'?"

"Yes, a youngster playing in his yard. He saw a man settin' a horse an' holding the reins on three others. He saw three men come out of an alley and mount up and then another man rode in from the street and they all trotted off down the lane.

"That youngster was nine years old, but canny. He noticed one of the horses. It was a black with three white feet and a white splash on the rump."

Borden Chantry put his cup down carefully. Then he looked across the table at Tyrel Sackett. "What are you sayin'?"

"I described a horse."

"I know you did, and I have a horse like that."

Sackett nodded. "I know you have. I saw him when I was down here right after Joe was killed. A mighty fine horse, too."

Borden Chantry took up his cup. His coffee was lukewarm, so he went to the stove for the coffeepot. He filled Sackett's cup, then his own. Returning the pot to the stovetop, he sat down, straddling his chair. "Sackett," he said slowly, "maybe we've got something. Let's run it into the corral and read the brands."

Chantry paused. "This here job was wished on me, but when it was offered I sure needed it. I'm no detective or even a marshal excep' by the wish of these folks in town. I went broke ranchin', Sackett. Drouth, rustlers, an' a bad market did me in, and when I was mighty hard up these folks asked me to be marshal. I've done my best."

"You solved the murder of my brother, Joe."

"Well, sort of. It was kind of like tracking strays. You know where the feed's best, where there might be water, an' where you'd want to go to hide from some dumb cowhand. It was just a matter of puttin' two an' two together."

"Like this."

"Sort of. You done any work on this?"

"A lot of riding an' thinking. Sort of like picking up the cards and shuffling them all together again, then dealing yourself a few hands faceup to see what the cards look like.

"Only in this case it wasn't cards, but news items." Tyrel Sackett reached in his breast pocket and brought out three clippings and spread them on the table facing Chantry.

All three were of holdups, and the dates were scattered over the last two years. Robberies, no shooting, no noise, no clues. The robbers appeared, then disappeared. One robbery was in Montana, one in Washington, one in Texas.

"Mighty spread out," Chantry commented. Only in Montana had there been an organized pursuit, and the bandits had switched to fresh horses and disappeared. "Had the horses waitin'," he commented.

"The rancher says no. They were horses he kept in his corral for emergencies, like going for a doctor or something like that."

"And somebody knew it."

Chantry looked over the descriptions. They were vague except for a tall, slim man wearing a narrow-brimmed hat.

"Funny-lookin' galoot" was the description of the man in the bank.

"I think he was meant to be," Sackett suggested. "I think he was meant to be noticed, like that man wearing the polka-dot shirt in Mora."

"You mean they *wanted* somebody to be able to describe him?" Chantry asked.

"Look at it. What happens is over in minutes, and

your attention focuses on the obvious. You're asked to describe the outlaws, and that polka-dot shirt stands out, or your tall man in the narrow-brimmed hat. You see the obvious and ignore the rest. You don't have a description, just a polka-dot shirt or a tall man in a narrow-brimmed hat. What were the others like? You don't recall. You've only a minute or two to look, so you see what's staring at you."

Chantry ran his fingers through his hair. "Sackett, until now I've been wonderin' if I'm foolish or not." He got up and walked to the sideboard and opened a drawer, taking out a sheaf of papers. "Looks like you an' me been tryin' to put a rope on the same calf."

He sat down and spread out the papers. They were wanted posters, letters, news clippings.

"Nine of them," he said, "Kansas, Arkansas, Wyoming, California, Texas, and Idaho. Two in California, three in Texas. Seven of them in the last four years, the others earlier. Nobody caught, no good descriptions, no clues.

"Nor were any strangers noticed hanging around town before the holdups. In four cases they got away without being seen so as to be recognized."

Chantry picked a wanted poster from the stack. "But look at this: *Four bandits, one described as a tall man wearing a Mexican sombrero*."

"The same man, with a different hat?"

"Why not?"

Sackett finished his coffee. "All over the West, the same pattern, clean getaways, and nobody saw anything."

Borden Chantry nodded toward the stack of papers. "Got two of those in the mail on the same day, and there seemed to be a similarity. I was comparing them when I remembered the wanted poster. Since then I been collecting these, and then I went over to the newspaper and went back through their files. They keep a stack of Denver and Cheyenne papers, too, so I ran a fairly good check."

Chantry got up and went over to the stove and, lifting the lid, glanced at the fire, then poked in a few small sticks, enough to keep the coffee hot.

"I'm glad you came over, Sackett. Now we've got to do some figuring."

"Let's start with your horse."

"You don't suspect me?"

Sackett smiled. "I suspect everybody, but I've got a theory. Suppose you tell me how you got him."

"It was roundup time, and it was late. Work had been held up and we got off to a bad start, so we were working our tails off when this gent came riding up to the chuck wagon leading five horses.

"He asked the cook if he could eat, and of course we fed him. I came in for coffee about that time, and he commented that we were shorthanded. I agreed, but added that what we were really short of was horses.

"He set there chewin' for a minute like he was thinkin' it over, and then he waved a hand at his stock. 'I've five head there you're welcome to use,' he said, 'all good stock horses. All I ask is that when you've finished the roundup you keep them up close to your house, in the corral or a small pasture where

I can pick 'em up when I come back through. An' keep 'em together.'

"That gent got up, threw his coffee grounds on the grass, and started for his horse. 'When will you be back?' I ask him, an' he says he's ridin' on to the coast and it may be six months or even a year, but don't worry. He'll be back. Maybe if we're drivin' stock we may just leave the horses we're ridin' an' pick up these. He turned his horse around and said, 'Treat 'em gentle. They're good stock.' An' he rode away.

"Those horses made all the difference, and so when we finished the roundup I did like he said, only once in a while I'd catch one of them up and ride him to town, like that black.

"That sort of thing isn't that unusual, and I gave it no thought until after they appointed me town marshal. When I was cleanin' out my desk over in the office I come on this reward poster. Seems like there'd been a holdup over east of here, just a few days before.

"Our newspaper wasn't operatin' then, and I'd been too busy tryin' to make ends meet, and nobody had mentioned any holdup to me.

"Four or five men, they said. Nobody seemed right sure. Well, I filed it with the others and gave it no thought, but I was roundin' up and sellin' off some of my own cows, tryin' to pay bills, and ridin' past my horse pasture I saw those five horses were gone but there were five others in their place.

"Five horses, all good stock, but they looked like

they'd been used mighty hard, an' just lately. That's when I started puttin' it all together."

The fire crackled in the stove, and the clock ticked in the silent room. Neither man spoke for some time. "Smart," Sackett said, at last. "Somebody is all-fired smart."

"How could they guess that a two-bit, rawhide rancher like me would someday be marshal?" Chantry said.

Sackett answered, "And they plan, they plan way ahead, like with your horses and that note of Orrin's." He gestured toward the papers. "There's twelve holdups or more, an' who knows anything?"

"I wonder how long it's been goin' on?"

Sackett shrugged. "Who knows? Or how many other robberies there have been of which we have no record? It would be my guess this is only the fringe. We're only two men in two mighty small towns." He tapped the stack of papers with his finger. "This makes the James boys look like pikers."

"They were pikers," Chantry said. "They advertised themselves too much. Everybody knew who they were, and they were two bloody, too many people killed for no reason, like that schoolboy who ran across the street in front of them."

"They've been getting away with this for years," Sackett commented, "but when they picked you to keep some horses for them they made their mistake. It only takes one."

"So what do we do now?"

Sackett indicated the stack of papers. "We go through that and look for something common to all of them. That tall man, for instance, who wears funny hats. And we write to places where there have been holdups. We look for some item common to them all, and there will be something."

"We've already got something," Chantry said. "We've got one thing, anyway."

"What's that?"

"Utah. There have been no robberies in Utah."

CHAPTER 4

BORDEN CHANTRY GOT to his feet, stood there for a moment thinking, then went over to a big, hide-covered chair and dropped into it.

"You think they're Mormons?"

"No," Sackett replied, "I don't. Most Mormons I've known were law-abiding folks, although there's a bad apple in every basket.

"But look at it like this: there's thousands of square miles of rough, wild country in southeastern Utah and neighboring parts of Colorado, Arizona, and New Mexico.

"This outfit seems to be operating all over the West, so why not Utah? My guess is he doesn't want trouble on his own doorstep."

He tapped the clippings. "Look here, a robbery in Montana and a day later, in Texas. That means, if we're figuring this right, that he has more than one bunch of men. My guess would be five or six, and to control that number of men and keep them disciplined their boss man has got to be both tough and smart. So far we haven't tied this outfit to a single killing, nor has anybody caught one of them."

Chantry studied the man at the table. He had heard all the stories, as had everyone. Tyrel Sackett was known to be one of the most dangerous gun-fighters in the West, a quiet young man who had come out from Tennessee, never hunting trouble, yet never backing away from it, either. Chantry had met Tyrel before when investigating the murder of his brother, Joe, but Sackett made him uncomfortable. He did not want such men, no matter how law-abiding, in his town. They had a way of attracting trouble.

He himself had never had the reputation of being a good man with a gun, yet deep inside him he was confident he could handle the best of them. He had not wanted to be a peace officer, yet when he needed money the job had been there, and he had accepted it.

Keeping the peace in a small western town was not that hard. Most of the cowboys who came into town and went on a drunk were men he had worked with. Some had worked for him, and some had worked trail drives and roundups beside him, so they were prepared to listen to him when he suggested they sleep it off.

He had been successful so far, but he made no claims to being a good officer. He was, well . . . he was competent. Up to a point, anyway. This job Sackett was talking about was out of his depth. He said as much.

Sackett gave him one of his rare smiles. "You're better than you think." He tapped the papers on the table. "You saw these and smelled something wrong. You've got an instinct for the job, Bord, whether you think so or not."

He tapped the papers again. "You know what we've got here? Something nobody would or will believe. Holdups are by local gangs, cowboys who need drinking money, something like that. By the very nature of them folks are going to say such men can't be organized. My guess is that in the last four years this outfit has pulled over a hundred holdups and robberies, gettin' away with every one.

"Somebody has to come in and scout the layout, somebody has to plan the getaway, somebody has to be sure there are fresh horses where they'll be needed."

"I don't know." Chantry shook his head. "Somewhere, somehow, something's got to give."

Sackett took out a billfold and extracted a news clipping. "They've had their troubles. Look at this."

SUSPECT ARRESTED AT CARSON

A man who gave his name as Dan Cable was arrested last night at Jennings' Livery. He had in his possession sacks containing $12,500 in freshly minted gold coin. He stated that he was en route to buy cattle.

Three days ago the bank at Rapid City was robbed of $35,000 in freshly minted gold coins. Cable is being held for investigation.

"So?"

"The next morning his cell was empty. He was gone, the gold was gone, his horse was gone. Nobody knows how it was managed."

"They moved fast," Chantry said thoughtfully. "They must have had somebody close by."

"There was no jailer at Carson. Small jail. The same key opens both the cell door and the outer door. Left alone like that he might have managed it himself."

"The gold?"

"Left in the desk drawer at the jail. The door was locked and it seemed safe. They'd had no trouble at Carson and the bank was closed, so the marshal just locked it up and left it.

"Carson's quiet now, so the two saloons close at midnight. After that the streets are empty. Cable just unlocked his door somehow, broke into the desk, then unlocked the outer door and went around to the livery stable, saddled his horse, and rode out."

"I'll be damned."

They talked until after midnight, carefully sifting the little they knew and going over the wanted posters, the news clippings, and a few letters from other peace officers and bankers.

"Maybe," Chantry said at last, "we'd better try to think ahead. If we could pick out several likely places we might beat them to it and be waiting."

"I thought of that. The trouble is there's so many possibilities. Of course, they'll be wanting a big strike."

"No stage holdups," Cantry suggested, "because when they carry big shipments they have a shotgun guard. Most of them will fight, so somebody is going to be killed."

Tyrel reached for the coffeepot and filled his cup.

"I've been thinkin' about what you said about tryin' to beat them to it." He paused. "How about right here? How about your town?"

Chantry shook his head. "The trouble with that is nobody here has any big money. Nobody—" He stopped, then sat up slowly. "Yeah," he muttered, "maybe. Just maybe."

Chantry looked up at Sackett, at the table. "You heard about that deal?"

"Heard about it? Everybody has been talking about it. Old man Merlin bought cows from ever'body around and paid them in scrip. Merlin had several gunmen riding with him, and nobody dared argue the point, so he drove off half the cattle in the county.

"About a year ago, I think it was, young Johnny Merlin told everybody he was coming back to redeem that scrip, a hundred thousand dollars worth, and he'd pay off in gold. His old man may have been a highbinder, but young Johnny was going to do the right thing.

"Next month Johnny will be in town, and he'll have a hundred thousand in gold here to pay off."

"Bait for a trap," Chantry said. He glanced up. "Seven thousand dollars of that is coming to me," he said. "I wouldn't want anything to happen to it."

"All right," Tyrel said quietly, "it's you and me, then. That outfit seems to have good information, so don't tell anybody who might repeat it. Just you and me. You've a good deputy, but don't tell him until the day. I'll bring a man along, too, and we'll be waiting."

"I hope they try it," Chantry said grimly.

"They will, Bord. I'm bettin' on it. You still got some o' their horses in that pasture?"

"I have."

"They'll come, Bord. This time they will get a surprise."

IN THE MASSIVE stone house at the head of Toadstool Canyon, Ben Curry leaned his great weight back in his chair and stared broodingly at the valley below. The door stood open, and the day was a pleasant one, yet Ben Curry was not feeling pleasant.

His big face was as blunt and unlined as the rock from which the house was built, but the shock of hair above that leonine face had turned gray. No nonsense about it, he was growing old. Even such a spring as this did not bring the old fire to his veins again, and it had been long since he had himself ridden on one of the jobs he planned so shrewdly. It was time to quit.

Yet, for a man who all his life had made quick and correct decisions, he was uncertain now. For six years he had ruled supreme in this corner of the mountains and desert. For twenty years he had been an outlaw, and for fifteen of those twenty years he had commanded a bunch of outlaws that had grown until it was almost an empire in itself.

Six years ago he had moved to this remote country and created the stronghold from which he operated. Across the southern limit was the Grand Canyon of the Colorado, barring all approach from that direction. To the east, north, and west was wilderness, much of it virtually impassable unless one knew the trails.

Only at Lee's Ferry was there a known crossing, but further along was the little-known Crossing of the Fathers. Both places were watched, day and night.

There was one other crossing, of an entirely different sort, that one known only to Ben himself. It was his ace in the hole.

One law of the gang was never transgressed. There was to be no lawless activity in the Mormon country to the north. Mormons and Indians were left strictly alone and were, if not friends, at least not enemies. Both groups kept what they knew to themselves, as well as what they suspected. A few ranchers lived on the fringes, and they traded at stores run by the outlaws. They could buy supplies there closer to home and at cheaper prices than elsewhere. The trading posts were listening posts as well. Strangers in the area were immediately noticed—usually they stopped by the stores, and their presence was reported to Ben Curry.

Ben Curry had not made up his mind about Kerb Perrin. He knew the outlaw was growing restive, aware that Curry was aging and eager for the power that went with leadership. What would he do, and how would he react when Mike Bastian took over?

Well, Curry reflected grimly, that would be Mike's problem. He had been trained for it.

Old Ben himself was the bull of the herd, and Perrin was pawing dust, but what would he do when a strange young bull came in to take over? One who had not won his spurs on the outlaw trail?

That was why Ben had sent for Mike. It was time for Mike to go out on his first job. It would be big, sudden, and dramatic. It was also relatively foolproof. If brought off smoothly it would have an excellent effect on the gang.

There was a sharp knock on the door, and Ben Curry sat back in his chair, recognizing it. "Come in!" he bellowed.

He watched Perrin enter and close the door behind him, then cross the room to him with his quick, nervous steps, his eyes scanning the room to see if they were alone.

"Chief, the boys are restless. It's spring, and most of them are broke. Have you got something in mind?"

"A couple of things. Yes, it's about time for them to move out." He paused. "Are they all back?"

"Most of them. Of course, as you know some of them never left."

"I've got one or two that look to be really tough. Seems it might be good for the kid to try one."

"Oh?" Perrin's irritation was obvious. "You mean he'll go along?"

"I'm going to let him run it. The whole show. It will be good for him."

Kerb Perrin absorbed that. For the first time he began to seriously consider Mike Bastian. Until now the only rival for leadership if Curry stepped down was Molina. He knew little about Bastian except to see him ride in and out of camp. He hunted a lot, was often with Roundy, and he knew Bastian had sat in on some of the planning at times. Yet for some reason he had never considered him as vying for leadership.

Perrin had accepted the fact that there would be trouble with Rig Molina, but Bastian? He was the old man's adopted son, but—

A quick, hot anger surged through him. It was all he could do to keep his voice calm. "Do you think that's wise? How will the boys feel about a green kid leading them?"

"He knows what to do, and they'll find he's as trailwise and smart as any of them. This is a big job and a tough one."

"Who goes along?" Kerb paused. "And what job?"

"Maybe I'll let him pick 'em. Good practice for him. What job? I haven't decided. Maybe the gold train, or maybe a job over in eastern Colorado. It's one I've been thinking about for some time."

The gold train? To Kerb's way of thinking that should be his job. He had discovered it, reported it, dug out most of the background detail. It was the job *he* wanted. It was a shipment from gold mines high in the mountains, gold brought down by muleback to the railroad, rich beyond dream.

Months before, in laying out the plan for Curry, he had it vetoed. He had recommended killing every man jack of them. Burial nearby, no witnesses, nothing. The gold train would simply have vanished into thin air. And he could do it. He knew he could.

"Too bloody," Curry objected. "You're beginning to sound like Molina."

"Dead men can't talk," Perrin insisted.

Ben Curry nodded agreement. "Maybe not, but their families can. A thing like that wakes people up, stirs their curiosity. Whenever people are killed some others want revenge or justice or whatever they call it. Whenever gold disappears it starts everybody in the country to looking."

Curry drummed his fingers on the table, thinking. "No," he said finally, "we won't do it. Not that way."

Even then as he spoke Curry was thinking of the effect upon the men if he let Bastian pull it off. Perrin was too bloody. Bastian would not be. Moreover, he could probably come up with a plan.

Many of the men knew Bastian slightly. Some of them had helped to train him in various skills. Some of the older men were as proud of Mike as if he had been their own son. If he brought off this job his position in the gang would be established. Yet what of Perrin?

Now, much later, he thought again of giving the job to Bastian. It was big, the biggest in years.

Fury surged up within Perrin. Curry had no right to do this! The gold train was his job! He found it, he scouted it, and as for killing them, if Curry was squeamish he was not. A total washout, that was the way to go. And now he was being sidetracked for a kid! Curry was shoving Bastian down their throats!

His rage died, but in its place there was resolution. It was time he acted on his own. For too long he had done what the old man directed. If Curry wanted the kid to handle the gold train, he would pull the other one whether Curry liked it or not. Moreover, he would be throwing a challenge into Curry's teeth because he would plan this job without him. If there was to be a struggle for leadership let it begin here.

"He'll handle the job," Curry said. "He has been trained and he has the mind for it. You boys couldn't be in better hands."

Kerb Perrin left the stone house filled with a burning resentment, but also with a feeling of grim triumph. After years of taking orders he was going on his own. To hell with Ben Curry! He'd show him! He would show them all!

Yet a still small voice of fear was in him, too. What would Ben Curry do?

The thought made him shrink inside. He had seen the cold fury of Curry when aroused, and he had seen him use a gun.

He was fast, but was he as fast and accurate as Ben Curry?

In his innermost being Perrin doubted it. He shook off the doubt. He could beat him. He knew he could. Yet maybe it would not be necessary. There were other ways.

One thing he knew. He would have to do something about Ben Curry, and he would have to do it soon.

CHAPTER 5

MIKE BASTIAN STOOD before Ben Curry's table and the two men stared at each other.

Ben Curry was huge, bearlike, and mighty. His eyes were cool and appraising, yet there was kindliness in them, too. This was the son he had always wanted, tall, lithe, powerful in the shoulders, a child of the frontier grown to manhood, skilled in all the arts of the wilds, trained in every dishonest practice, every skill with weapons, but educated enough to conduct himself well in any company.

"Take four men and look over the ground yourself, Mike," Ben Curry was saying. "I want you to plan this one. The gold train leaves the mines on the twentieth. There will be five wagons, the gold distributed among them, roughly five hundred thousand dollars of it.

"We've scouted the trail three times over the past couple of years, so all you'll have to do is ride over it to be sure nothing has changed.

"Don't be seen if you can help it. Don't ask questions or loiter around anyplace where people are. If you speak to anybody ask how far it is to Prescott. Let 'em think you're just passin' through.

"When you've pulled off this job I'm goin' to step down and pass the reins to you. You'll be in command. You've known I intended to do this for some years now.

"I'm gettin' up there in years, and I want a few years of quiet life. This outfit takes a strong hand to run it. Think you can handle it?"

"I think so."

"I think so, too. Watch Perrin. He's got a streak of snake in him. Rigger is dangerous, but whatever he does will be out in the open. It's not that way with Perrin. He's a conniver. He never got far with me because I was always a jump ahead of him, and I still am!"

Curry fell silent, staring out the window at the distant peaks of the San Francisco mountains.

"Mike," he said, more quietly, "sit down. It's time you an' me had a talk. Maybe I've taken the wrong trail with you, raisin' you the way I have, to be an outlaw an' all.

"I'm not sure what's right an' what's wrong, an' to tell the truth, I never gave much thought to it. When I came west it was dog eat dog and if you lived you had to have big teeth. I got knocked down and kicked around some. Cattlemen pushed me off the first homestead I staked, and killed my sister.

"When I struck it rich in the mines some men moved in and took it away from me. They done it legal, but it wasn't right or just, so I decided it was time to bite back.

"I got some boys together, and when those fellers shipped gold from my claim we stole it back. Then I rode east and with a big outfit I moved in and ran off five hundred head of stock from that outfit that pushed me off my homestead.

"They took in after me and I let the boys take the cattle over into Mexico and I went back and ran off another five hundred head whilst they were chasing the first batch. When I had those cattle started south with some of the boys I went back and pulled down his corrals, and stamped my brand on the door of his house. I mean, I burned it deep. I wanted him to know who hit him.

"They taken in after me, the law did. They wanted me in prison, but I stayed clear of them. Now I was an outlaw, whether I liked it or not, and stamping that brand on his door had been a fool thing to do.

"That's the trouble with outlaws, they want to brag about what they've done. Well, I'd made my mistake but decided I would never do that again.

"So all these years we've kept quiet about what we were doin'. My boys move in, get what they came after, and drop from sight. Those James boys now, ever'body knows who they are, so they have to stay hid out most of the time."

He paused. "Who you want to take with you? I mean to do your scouting?"

"Roundy, Doc Sawyer, Colley, and Garlin."

Curry nodded slowly, then looked over at him. "Why?"

"Roundy has an eye for terrain like nobody in this country. He says mine's as good, but I'd like him along. Doc Sawyer is completely honest, and if he thinks I'm wrong he'll say so. As for Colley and Garlin, they are two of the best men in the outfit. They will be pleased if I ask their help, which may put them on my side when I need them."

Curry nodded. "That's good thinking. Yes, Colley and Garlin are two of our best men, and if there's trouble later with Molina an' Perrin, it will be good to have them on your side."

Later, when Bastian had gone, Ben Curry got up and walked to the window. He was feeling restless and irritable and he did not know why, unless—

For the first time he was having doubts as to his course of action. What right did he have to start Mike down the outlaw trail? Maybe Roundy was right, and the time for all that was over and past. The country was filling up and the old days were fading. Even the Indians were settling down, unwillingly perhaps, but settling nonetheless. For several years past he had been careful in picking the spots for his boys to operate. Some of the small-town marshals were very tough men, and the townspeople were changing, too. Just look what happened to the James boys up there in Minnesota, shot to pieces by a bunch of farmers and businessmen.

Bill Chadwell, Clell Miller, and Charlie Pitts had been killed, all three of the Youngers wounded and one of them so bad he could travel no further. Jesse had wanted to shoot him and leave him behind but the Youngers stood by their brother, so Jesse and Frank had gone off by themselves. And one of them wounded.

The James boys had gotten a lot of sympathy because they were supposed to be still fighting for the Lost Cause. That just wouldn't wash because most of the banks they robbed were southern banks operated by former Confederates or other southerners.

Ben Curry turned away from the window and walked to the fireplace. Picking up his pipe from the mantel, he knocked out the ashes and refilled the pipe.

Hell, he had trained the boy for what he was to do, and he would be handling a couple of hundred of the toughest men around. Although, come to think of it, the time was coming when the outfit should be cut down in size. Some of the boys didn't take to this life. They liked to drink and carouse more, and they wanted to spend their money as fast as they made it.

He thought back to Mora. Despite his scoffing at Roundy's worries, he was having doubts himself.

Tyrel Sackett? He had heard the boys talking about him but had paid little attention. After all, they were always talking about some gunfighter, some bucking horse, or something of the kind. Yet Roundy was right, he had been back in the hills too much. He was losing touch.

That little town in Colorado, now? That should be an easy touch. Maybe he should start the kid on that one? And he had left some horses there with a rancher. Big, strong-looking man, ranching a rawhide outfit.

He relit his pipe. He would have to watch Kerb Perrin. Perrin had not liked it a bit when he had suggested Mike to handle the treasure train. Perrin had not said much, but he knew him all too well.

Kerb Perrin was dangerous. Perrin was shrewd, a conniver and a plotter, good at planning but apt to fly off the handle. He was given to impatience and sudden rages. Frustration infuriated him.

MIKE BASTIAN WAS EXCITED. At twenty-two he had been considered a man for several years, but in all that time except for a few trips to Salt Lake City he had rarely left the mountain and canyon country where he had grown up.

Roundy led the way, for the trail was a familiar one to him, an old Indian trail the outlaws used when they rode out of the country to the south.

Snow still lay in some of the shadowed places, but as they neared the canyon the cliffs towered even higher and the trail dipped into a narrow gorge with sheer rock walls that gave way to rolling red waves of solid rock enlivened by the green of scattered cedar that seemed to grow right from the rock itself.

In this wild country, seeing another human, even an Indian, was a rare thing. The Navajo country lay south of them, and there were still a few scattered Paiutes, who probably knew this country better than anyone. Ben Curry had established a friendship with them right from the start, traded horses with them, left them occasional presents, and kept his men away from their camps.

Mike followed Roundy, riding hump-shouldered on his ragged gray horse that seemed as old as himself but was mountain-wise and reliable in any kind of a pinch.

Behind them rode Doc Sawyer, his lean, saturnine features showing little of what he thought, his eyes always alert and faintly amused. Tubby Colley was short, thick-chested, and confident, a hard-jawed man who had been a first-rate ranch foreman before he killed two men and had to hit the outlaw trail.

Tex Garlin was tall, rangy, and quiet. Little was known of his background aside from the fact that he came from Texas, although it was said that if he had been that kind he might have carved a dozen notches on his gun.

Roundy turned his horse around a gray boulder and struck a dim trail along the face of the cliff, following a route that led them right down to the river.

There was a small cabin and a square plot of garden. The door opened and a man awaited them with a rifle. His cold old eyes went from one to the other. "Howdy! I been expectin' comp'ny." His eyes went to Mike Bastian. "Ain't seen him before."

"It's all right," said Roundy. "This is Ben Curry's boy."

"Heard of you. Can you shoot like they say?"

Mike flushed. "I don't know what they say, but I'll bet a lot of money I can hit the side of that mountain if it will hold still."

"Don't take no funnin' from him," Roundy said. "If he has to, he can shoot."

"Let's see some shootin', son," the old man said. "I always did like to see a man who can shoot."

Bastian shook his head. "A man's a fool to shoot

unless there's reason. Ben Curry taught me never to draw a gun unless I meant to use it."

"Go ahead," Colley urged. "Show us."

The old man pointed. "See that black stick over there? That's about fifty, maybe sixty paces. Could you hit that?"

The stick was no wider than a piece of lath, barely discernible against the backdrop of rock. "You mean that one?" Mike Bastian palmed his gun and fired and the end of the black stick pulverized.

The move was so smooth and practiced that no one of the men even guessed he intended to shoot. Garlin's jaws ceased their methodical chewing and he stared as long as it would take to draw a breath. He glanced at Colley, spat, and said, "I wonder what Kerb Perrin would say to that?"

Colley nodded. "Yeah," he said softly, "but the stick wasn't shootin' back at him."

Old Bill took them over the swollen river in one hair-raising trip, and with the river behind them they started south. Several days later, after exchanging horses at several points along the way and checking the stock available at each stop, they rode into the little mining town of Weaver.

Colley and Garlin rode in about sundown, followed an hour or so later by Roundy and Doc Sawyer. They kept apart, and when Mike Bastian rode in alone he did not join the others.

Most of those gathered in the saloon were Mexicans who kept to themselves, but there were three tough-looking white men at the bar whom Mike eyed warily.

One of them glanced at Mike in his beaded buckskins and whispered something to the others, at which they all laughed.

Mike leaned nonchalantly at the bar, avoiding the stares of the three men. One of them moved closer to him.

"Hi, stranger! That's a right purty suit you got there. Where can I get one like it?"

Garlin heard and glanced over at Colley. "Corbus an' Fletcher! And trouble hunting! Maybe we should get into this."

"Wait, let's see how the kid handles it."

Mike's expression was mild. "You want an outfit like this? Almost any Indian can make one for you." He had taken their measure at once and knew the kind of men he had to deal with. There is at least one such in every bar. Given a few drinks they hunt trouble.

"Just that easy?" Corbus asked.

He was in a quarrelsome mood, and Mike looked too neat for his taste.

Trouble was coming and there was no way to avoid it. If he walked out they would follow him. It was better to meet it head-on. "Just like that," Mike said, "but I don't know what you'd want with it. A suit like this would be too big for you."

"Huh?" Corbus was startled by the brusque tone. "You gettin' smart with me, kid?"

"No," Mike replied coolly, "nor am I about to be hurrahed by any lamebrain, whiskey-guzzling saddle tramp.

"You commented on my suit and I told you where

you could get one. Now you can have a drink on me, all three of you, and I'm suggesting we drink up." His voice became softer. "I want you to have a drink because I want to be very, very sure we're friends, see?"

Corbus stared at Bastian, a cold hint of danger filtering through. This might be dangerous going, but he was stubborn, too stubborn to laugh it off and accept the drink and end the trouble. "Suppose I don't want to drink with no tenderfoot brat?"

Corbus never saw what happened. His brain warned him as Bastian's left hand moved, but he never saw the right. The left smashed his lips, and the right cracked on the angle of his jaw. He hit the floor on his shoulder blades, out cold.

Fletcher and the third tough hesitated. Corbus was on the floor and Bastian was not smiling. "You boys want a drink or do we go on from here?"

"What if a man drawed a gun instead of usin' his fists?" Fletcher asked.

"I'd kill him," Mike replied.

Fletcher blinked. He had been shocked sober by what happened to Corbus. "I reckon you would. All right, let's have that drink. The boot hill out there already has twenty graves in it."

Relieved, the bartender poured. Nobody looked at Corbus, who was still out.

"What will Corbus do when he gets up?" Colley wondered.

Garlin chuckled. "Nothing today. He won't feel like it."

There was silence and then Garlin said, "I can't

wait to see Kerb Perrin's face when he hears of it."
He glanced over at Colley. "There's a whisper goin'
around that the old man intends the kid to take over."

"That is the rumor."

"Well, he can shoot and he doesn't waste around.
Maybe he can cut the mustard."

Mike Bastian finished his beer as he heard a stage
roll into the street. It offered an easy way out and he
took it, following several men who started for the
door.

The passengers were getting down to stretch their
legs and eat. There was a boardinghouse alongside
the saloon. Three of the passengers were women, all
were well dressed, with an eastern look to them.

Seeing him, one of the younger women walked up
to him. She was a pale, pretty girl with large gray
eyes. "What is the fastest route to Red Wall Canyon?" she asked.

Mike Bastian was suddenly alert. "You will make
it by morning if you ride the stage. There is a cross-
country route if you have a buckboard."

"Could you show us where to hire one? My
mother is not feeling well."

Doc Sawyer was on the steps behind him. "Be
careful, Mike," he spoke softly. "This could be trouble."

CHAPTER 6

MIKE STEPPED DOWN into the street and walked back to the stage with her. The older woman and the other girl were standing near the stage, but he had eyes only for the girl.

Her hair seemed to have a touch of gold but was a shade or two darker than the hair of the girl who had spoken to him. She who had approached him was quiet and sweet. This other girl was vivid.

Their eyes met and he swept off his hat. The girl beside him spoke. "This is my mother, Mrs. Ragan, and my sister, Drusilla." She looked up at him. "I am Juliana."

Mike bowed. He had eyes only for Drusilla. "I am Mike Bastian," he replied.

"He said we could hire a rig to take us by a shorter route to Red Wall Canyon."

"Just where in the canyon did you wish to go?" he asked.

"To the V-Bar, Voyle Ragan's place."

He had started to turn away, but stopped in mid-stride. "Did you say—Voyle Ragan's?"

"Yes. Is there anything wrong?"

"No, no. Of course not. I just wanted to be sure."
He smiled. "I wanted to be sure. I might want to
come calling."

Juliana laughed. "Of course! We would be glad to
see you. It gets rather lonely at the ranch sometimes,
although we love it. Sometimes I think I could spend
the rest of my life there."

Mike walked swiftly away, heading for the livery
sign he had seen along the street. These then were
Ben Curry's wife and daughters, and somehow Doc
Sawyer knew it. How many others knew?

He was their foster brother, but obviously his
name was unknown to them. Nor would he have
guessed who they were but for what Roundy had
told him. Yet he was, as Sawyer had warned, treading
on dangerous ground. He must reveal nothing of
what he knew, either to them or anyone else. This
was Ben Curry's secret and he was entitled to it.

Hiring the rig was a matter of minutes, and he
liked the looks of the driver, an older man with a
lean, weathered face and an air of competence about
him.

"No danger on that road this time of year," the
driver said. "I can have them there before the stage is
more than halfway. I don't have to take that round-
about route to pick up passengers."

"Take good care of them," Bastian said.

He left while the man was harnessing his team and
walked back to the boardinghouse.

Drusilla looked up as he came in. "Did you find a
rig?"

"He'll be around in a matter of minutes. It will be

a long drive but you could lie down in the back if you like. He was putting in some buffalo robes when I left."

"You're very kind."

"I hope I am," he said, "but all I could think of was that you were beautiful."

She blushed, or seemed to. The light wasn't very good.

"And I can come to visit?"

"My sister invited you, didn't she?"

"Yes, but I'd like the invitation from you, too."

"All right. Now why don't you ask my mother, too? She likes visitors as much as Julie and I do."

"I'll have to take the invitation from you and your sister as being enough. If I ask your mother I might have to ask your father, too."

"He isn't with us. His name is Ben Ragan and he is probably off buying cattle or looking at mining property. He travels a great deal. Do you know him?"

"I've heard the name," he said.

He sat with them, eating a little, drinking coffee, and listening to them talking of the trip. Drusilla was very cool, saying little. Twice he caught her eyes upon him but each time she looked away, though without embarrassment.

"You won't be able to see much but stars," he said. "My advice is to lie down in the back and get what rest you can."

"Do you live over that way?" Juliana asked.

"Sort of," he said, "when I'm home." He hesitated, not wanting to lie. "I've always been a kind of hunter, so I keep to the wild country." He paused, thinking that being a hunter did not seem like much of a life to such girls as these. "I'm thinking of going into ranching."

Drusilla glanced at him coolly, curiously. She was disturbing, in more ways than one. Did she believe him? Why did she look at him like that?

When they had gone he walked back to the saloon, dissatisfied more than ever. At the bar he listened to the talk and had another beer. All such places were clearinghouses for information. Men did business there, found jobs, sought entertainment, often even attended church services in saloons. Certainly, if one wanted to know what was happening in the country, that was the place to go.

There was talk of the gold shipment as men were being hired to make the trip. The guards, he heard, had been chosen. Now, more than ever, it seemed fantastic that he could actually be planning to steal all that gold, with the possibility of resistance, of even killing men.

He considered that. Killing a man in a fair fight was something that could happen to anyone, but killing men who were defending property was something else. He stared gloomily into his beer. What would Drusilla think of that? And what would Ben Curry think of an outlaw visiting his daughters?

The idea that he might someday lead the gang had been with him for years. He knew he had been trained for it, conditioned for it. He knew Curry had based all his plans on him, Mike Bastian. So now what?

Often he had thought of what he would do and

how he would do it. He supposed many a man had considered a holdup and how it should be done but with no idea of ever doing it. It was a form of daydreaming, but with no connection to reality. The trouble was this was no longer a daydream, this *was* reality. Now, suddenly, he was uneasy.

Yet he was thinking not only of himself but of Drusilla.

What a girl she was! And her father was an outlaw. Was she aware of it? He doubted that. Roundy said Ben Curry had kept his family life completely away from his other side. Ben Curry himself was a strange man, one who, had he gone straight, might have directed his energies into cattle, mining, or some other business, even into politics. He knew men and had a genius for organization and control. A strange life, turned off suddenly down the wrong roads. But that was Ben Curry. What of him? What of Mike Bastian?

Doc Sawyer cashed in his chips and strolled to the bar, offering to buy him a drink. It was a casual meeting, like many that occur in saloons.

"The twentieth," he said, "and there will be five shotgun guards, but twelve guards in all. The big fellow at the poker table is one of them." He paused. "It looks bad, Mike. It looks very bad, indeed."

What Roundy said was true, of course. He was still an honest man. This was the turning point. Once he stepped over that boundary that separated the thieves from honest men it would not be the same. Of course, later he might be able to step out of it as Ben Curry would do. If he was able to do it.

Listening to Sawyer made him wonder. Why had such a man, brilliant, intelligent, and a skilled surgeon, why had he taken to the outlaw trail?

"Doc"—he spoke softly—"whatever made you take this route?"

Sawyer glanced at him. "Having doubts, Mike?"

"Doubts? It seems all I have these days are doubts."

"I've wondered about that. You've said nothing, so I assumed you were perfectly willing to go along with Ben's plans for you.

"It means power and money, Mike. If it is the future for outlaws that disturbs you, don't let it. From now on it will be different than in Ben Curry's day. You will have to have the best lawyers, the right connections, and spend some money for bribes, but with the money you will have that should be easy.

"Roundy told me he had spoken to you about it. He can see it more clearly than Ben. The old days are over. Up to now all those robberies were considered to have been pulled off by free-wheeling outfits like the James boys and the Renos. Nobody has thought there might be an organization behind it. That will change. There are some pretty shrewd officers out there and when they begin getting organized themselves outlaws will have no chance. Still, with the connections, the lawyers, and the money you should manage."

"Yes, it could be," Mike agreed. "Only maybe I don't want it that way."

Sawyer smiled wryly. "Does conscience rear its ugly head? Can it be that Ben Curry's conditioning has fallen on fallow ground? What started this sudden feeling? Is it fear? Or a woman?"

"Would that be so strange?"

"That it was a woman? I've wondered it hasn't happened before, except that you've been such a recluse. If it is a woman, take a second look and time to think about it."

"It wasn't her. I've been thinking about it for the past two years. I've been wondering what I should do. I hate to disappoint Ben Curry, and actually, I've no other place to go. What can I do? Hunt? Punch cows?"

Doc Sawyer put his glass down hard. "Either is better, Mike. Anything is better. And it's easier to get in than get out. Once you have the name, it follows you.

"But don't ask me. I made a mess of my own life. Partly a woman and partly for what I thought would be easy money. Well, let me tell you, there's no such thing as easy money. You make your own decision. What was it Matthew Arnold said, I think you learned the quotation."

" 'No man can save his brother's soul, or pay his brother's debt.' "

"That's it! You save your own and you pay your own. But remember this, Mike. No matter which way you go, there will be killing. If you take over from Ben you'll have to kill either Kerb Perrin or Rig Molina, maybe both of them. And if you decide to step out you may have to kill them and even Ben Curry."

"Oh, no! Not Pa!"

"Mike, get this through your head. There is no easy way out. Do you suppose you're alone in this? Roundy an' me have talked this up one side and down the other. After all," he added, "neither of us ever had a son. We've helped to train you and teach you, and it has meant a lot to us.

"But remember this. No man is a complete ruler or dictator. He is only the mouthpiece for the wishes of his followers. As long as he expresses those wishes, he leads them.

"Ben is the boss because he is strong, because he has organization, because he is good with those guns. Also he is boss because he has made them money, kept them out of trouble, sometimes even against their own wishes. He has offered them security. If you walked out there would be a chink in the armor. No outlaw ever trusts another who turns honest. He always fears betrayal."

"Let's check with Roundy."

He was coming across the room to them. "Get the horses. We've got to blow town. Ducrow and Fernandez just rode in, and they are drunk and they are talking. If they see us they are apt to spill everything."

Garlin was there. "Ducrow's a pal of Perrin's. He thinks he can get away with anything."

"Here they come now!"

"All right! Drift!" Bastian ordered. "Be quick with the horses!"

CHAPTER 7

THE WORLD OF most criminals is incredibly small, consisting largely of others like himself. He wants to be considered a big man, a tough man, a smart man among his own kind. If not that, he wants to be associated with somebody who is big, tough, and smart, even if only to run errands for him.

Few can stand alone, most are afraid to try. The gang is their protection and their strength. It is also their refuge.

Their world is a few hangouts, a few saloons, a few places where the lawbreakers meet. If in the city it comprises a few city blocks, in the western lands a few towns, a few hundred square miles of territory. When escaping they will almost invariably return to old associations, to areas they know, people with whom they are familiar.

Ben Curry had provided the refuge, the planning, access to money, but most of his men did not like it. They were restless for freedom, to go as they pleased, act as they wished. Most of them wanted the reputation of being bad men, they wished to swagger and strut. Over the years Ben had tried to weed them out, to keep the cool and careful men, to eliminate the braggarts and the show-offs. He had only been partially successful.

Usually he managed to weed out the undesirables before they knew anything about the ramifications of his operations. Ducrow had been a tough man, a quiet man, but lately he had become a close ally of Perrin. Also, he had begun drinking too much.

Saloon doors slammed open and the two men came in. One glance and Mike knew there was trouble, not only for him but for Ben Curry, all of them. Tom Ducrow was drunk and ugly. Behind him was Snake Fernandez. An unpleasant pair, they had made trouble before this, always protected by Perrin.

Bastian started toward them but had taken scarcely a step when Ducrow saw him. "There he is! The pet! The boss's pet!"

"Tom," Bastian said mildly, "I'd suggest you go sleep it off. This isn't the place."

"Look who's givin' orders! Gettin' big for your britches, ain't you?"

"Your horses will be outside the door," Bastian suggested. "Get on them and start for home."

Ducrow planted his feet. "Suppose you make me!"

"Tom," Mike protested, "this isn't the place!" He stepped closer and lowered his voice. "Ben wants no trouble, you know that."

"Ben? Who the hell is Ben? Kerb Perrin's the man, an' don't you forget it!"

It was a challenge, and more words might reveal too much. Mike Bastian struck swiftly. A left to the body, a right to the chin. Ducrow was not a fistfighter and the blows were totally unexpected. He went to his knees, then slumped facedown to the floor.

With an oath, Fernandez went for his gun and Mike had no choice. He shot him through the shoulder. The gun dropped from Snake's fingers. Mouthing curses, he reached for his left-hand gun. Garlin, who had stayed behind when the others went for their horses, grabbed him from behind and disarmed him.

Mike pulled the groggy Ducrow to his feet and started for the door.

He found himself facing a big man with a stern look and a star on his chest. "What's going on here?" he demanded.

Mike smiled pleasantly. "Nothing at all, Officer. A couple of boys from our outfit with too much red-eye. We'll take them back to camp and we're moving out in the morning."

The sheriff looked from Mike to Doc Sawyer. The apparent respectability of the two calmed him somewhat. "Who are you? I don't know you."

"No, sir. We've come up from the Mogollons, driving a few head of cattle to a ranch in California. It has been a rough trip and the boys got a little too much to drink."

The sheriff was suspicious. There was something here he did not understand. "You may be a cowhand," he said, "but that gent with you looks like a gambler!"

Mike chuckled. "Officer, I've played with him, and if he had to make his living with cards he'd starve. As a matter of fact, he's a doctor, a surgeon, and a mighty good one. He's a friend of the boss."

A tall, gray-haired man had strolled over beside the sheriff. "What outfit did you say you rode for? I'm from the Mogollons, myself."

Garlin had hustled Fernandez and Ducrow outside as they talked. Doc Sawyer was wishing he had gone with them.

"I don't ride for a Mogollon outfit," Mike said, smiling, "but Jack McCardle can vouch for me. Doc Sawyer is a friend of his and has handled the sale of some of his beef."

The sheriff glanced at the gray-haired man. "Do you know this McCardle, Joe?"

"I do, and he's a good man. He has the Flying M, but I didn't know he was selling cattle."

"Guess you're all right." The sheriff was reluctant to let go. He studied Mike. "You sure don't talk like no cowhand."

"Officer, cowhands come from everywhere and anywhere. We had a puncher working with us last year from Norfolk, England. However," he said gravely, "I was studying for the ministry but my interests led me in more profane directions. I am afraid I'm a backslider. An interest in draw poker isn't conducive to a place in the pulpit."

"I guess not." The sheriff chuckled. "All right, you ride out of here, but no more trouble, do you hear? And Doc, you better look at that man's shoulder."

Mike turned away and Doc followed. Outside, the men had disappeared. They rode out of town, heading north. It was not until they were several miles on the road that Doc rode up beside Bastian.

"You'll do!" he said. "You handled that better than anybody I know."

"Hell!" Garlin said. "I was gettin' ready to shoot our way out of town. You sure smooth-talked 'em!"

"That sheriff," Mike said thoughtfully, "wasn't satisfied. He'll ride out come daybreak and check for tracks."

Garlin chuckled. "I figured on it. We're ridin' somebody's cow trail right now. I seen 'em passin' when we rode into town. I figure they were headed for a grassy patch with a spring about four mile west, and they'll be gone by daybreak. I doubt if that sheriff is ready to ride that far just to check up on us."

KERB PERRIN AND RIG MOLINA were sitting around the table in the stone house when Mike and Doc returned to the canyon. Both men looked up sharply, and Ben Curry was suddenly watchful.

Bastian wasted no time. "Kerb, what were Ducrow and Fernandez doing in Weaver?"

Perrin looked around, irritated by Mike's tone but puzzled, too.

"In Weaver! And drunk! We nearly had to shoot our way out of town because of them. They were drunk and talking too much. When I told them to get on their horses and head for home, they made trouble."

"How?"

"Ducrow was attracting too much attention. If I

hadn't stopped him there's no telling what he'd have said."

"*You* stopped him?"

Ben Curry had leaned back in his chair and was watching with attention.

"I knocked him out," Mike said coolly, "and when Fernandez went for his gun I put a bullet into his shoulder."

"You should've killed him," Molina said. "You'll have it to do sooner or later."

Kerb Perrin was stumped. This was something he had not wanted to happen, nor would he have believed Mike Bastian could handle Ducrow, let alone Fernandez as well.

"We got what we went after," Bastian told Curry, "but another break like we had and we'll walk into a trap. As for that, I think we should drop it for now."

"Are you crazy?" Perrin said. "That's the big one. That's the one we've been waiting for!"

"The sheriff in Weaver," Mike said, "is a good man, a tough man, and a smart one. I talked our way out of it, but he may do some checking. He struck me as a careful man."

"To hell with him!" Perrin said.

When Perrin and Molina had gone, Mike left for his own room and Doc Sawyer turned to Ben. "It would have done your heart good! He had a run-in with Corbus and Fletcher, too! He flattened Corbus with a punch and backed Fletcher down. He'll do, that boy of yours!"

"I knew he had it," Ben said, with satisfaction.

"He met a girl, too," Doc added.

"Good for him! It's about time."

"This was a very particular girl, Chief. If I am any judge of such things he fell and fell hard, and I'm not sure it didn't happen both ways."

Something in his tone caught Curry's attention. "Who was she?"

"A girl who came in on the stage. Mike got her and her family a rig and a driver to take them to their ranch. Out to the V-Bar."

Ben Curry turned on him. For a moment their eyes held. So Doc Sawyer knew! The one secret he had been determined to keep, the one he wanted none of them to know! How many others knew? How many had guessed? Or discovered some clue? And he had believed his tracks had been covered. For the first time Ben Curry knew fear, real fear.

"The girl's name is Drusilla Ragan. She's a beautiful girl, Ben."

"I won't have it!" Ben slammed his glass down. "I'll be damned if—!"

Doc Sawyer's tone was ironic. "You mean the foster son you raised isn't good enough for your daughter?"

"Don't use that word here! Who knows besides you?"

"Nobody of whom I know. It is only accident that I know. Remember the time you were laid up with that bullet wound, and I took care of you myself? You were delirious, and you talked too much." Doc lighted his pipe. "They made a nice-looking couple," he added, "and I believe she invited him to Red Wall Canyon."

"He won't go! I'll not have any of this crowd there! If you think I want my daughter associating with outlaws—!"

"He isn't—yet." Doc puffed on his pipe. "He could be, and he might be, but if he does, the crime will be on your shoulders because I don't think he wants to be."

Curry went to the window and looked down the canyon.

"Chief, the boy has it in him. He could be all of it, believe me! He's quick! You should have seen him throw that gun on Fernandez! And when that sheriff walked up to him he handled it like a veteran!"

Ben Curry was silent. Doc glanced at the broad back and went over to the sideboard and took up a cup and filled it with coffee.

"He may be deciding he doesn't want to take over. That boy's smart, Ben, *smart*!"

"He'll do what I tell him."

"Maybe. He's got a mind of his own, Ben."

Ben swore under his breath. All his plans, all of it, falling apart after all the thinking, all the years!

A small voice of doubt was whispering within him, a voice that made him remember that quiet, determined little boy whom he brought home with him, that boy who would not cry, a boy who listened and obeyed and who tried very hard to do what was expected of him. Yet despite that Ben had always been aware the boy had a mind of his own, that he listened and weighed everything in some balance of his own.

Long after Doc Sawyer was gone, Ben Curry sat alone, thinking. If Doc knew, somebody else might know, yet he thought not. Doc was canny, and Doc always had his ear to the ground. Doc would know if anybody else knew.

HIS THOUGHTS REVERTED to the discussion over what had taken place in Weaver. What were Ducrow and Fernandez doing there, anyway? It had always been the policy for none of the gang to show up in the town where a job was to be pulled off except the scouts who went in, got the lay of the land, then rode out as unobtrusively as possible.

Now there had been trouble, attention had been drawn to them, and Ducrow had been drunk and shooting off his mouth. Mike warned that the sheriff was a canny man, and he would remember their faces. So none of them could be used. The boy was out of it.

Despite himself, Ben felt relief. The risk had worried him. Twelve guards, several with shotguns. How were they to handle *them*?

Kerb Perrin wanted the job, so let Kerb have it. For the first time the thought of betrayal entered his mind. He shook his head.

No. Perrin was his problem. He would cope with it himself, as he always had. But what were Ducrow and Fernandez doing in Weaver? And Doc had reported the words Ducrow had spoken in anger, that it was no longer Ben Curry who mattered, but Kerb Perrin.

Something brewing there.

He was getting old. For the first time he began to

doubt his rightness. What about the boy? He had wanted a man he could trust to take over, but had he any right to raise the boy to be an outlaw?

He walked to the window again. He had a reason, or thought he did, but Mike had none beyond his father's wish. Suddenly, Ben stopped, staring at the partial reflection of himself in the glass. Mike was the son he had never had, why not Mike and Drusilla?

He shook his head. No, no. Never. Yet—how many fathers could raise their own son-in-law? He smiled at the thought, but put it aside. There was too much else to think about now.

Kerb Perrin was planning rebellion. Planning to go his own way.

His thoughts reverted to Dru. Suppose she wanted Mike Bastian, outlaw or not? Had it been Juliana now, he could have bluntly told her no and she would have, might have, listened. But Dru? He chuckled. She would laugh at him. She was too much like him.

What to do? Ben Curry moved away from the window. He must remember not to stand there again. Once, he need not have worried but now there were enemies among his own men, something he dared not tolerate.

What had Ducrow and Fernandez been doing in Weaver? Scouting the job for Perrin? For themselves?

He walked back to the fireplace and stared at the sullen coals. He was growing old, and it was time to quit. He wanted the last years with his wife and the girls. He wanted to get out, to get away. He was a man born out of his time, and in the past he might have been a Viking, a robber baron, a freebooter. Now he was an outlaw.

He had liked planning their forays. He had liked playing his chess game with the law, but lately—

Was he changing? Or was it the times? Was it like Roundy kept telling him, that the old days were gone? An outlaw was an enemy of society, a different society from that rough, casually tolerant West in which he had spent his early years.

He walked over to the clothes tree and took down his gun-belt. He checked each pistol, then slung the belt about his hips.

From now on he had better wear them, all the time.

CHAPTER 8

M IKE BASTIAN ROLLED out of bed and sat up. Rarely did he sleep during the day, but on his return he had been tired. Now he felt better.

Darkness had come while he rested, and the sky was spangled with stars. From his window he could see a few lights glowing from the settlement below, a settlement of outlaws.

Only Doc Sawyer and himself shared the stone house with Ben Curry, and on the occasional visits when others discussed future jobs with Ben, they never left the spacious living room with its big table where the planning was done.

The doors leading to other rooms were closed and conferences were kept to the big table. Ben Curry had always been a private person and nobody had ever ventured to intrude on that privacy, not even Mike himself.

He was restless and uneasy. There had been a sampling of what he could expect in the facing of Corbus and later with Ducrow and Fernandez. Was that what he wanted? Or did he want a more respectable life? Such a life as Drusilla Ragan might wish to share?

Hey! He flushed. What was he thinking of? She had scarcely noticed him, and who was he, after all? He was nothing, he had nothing. He did not have a home, other than this provided by Ben Curry, he had no job, he had nothing to offer. Although he knew there were some people who admired outlaws, largely because they had never known any, he did not think Drusilla would be of that sort.

He had not needed Roundy's questions, nor Doc's, to start thinking. Whenever he went into a town he wondered about the people there. They did not have to worry about being recognized by some lawman or some former victim. They did not have to be hiding out in the hills, seeking shelter from cold and rain or suffering from a gunshot wound they dared not have treated.

Ben's operation was the most successful, but he had his failures, too. Only a few weeks before four of the boys had arrived on hard-ridden horses, one man wounded, with only fourteen dollars to show for their trouble. At the last minute, plans had been altered and the shipment of gold had gone out early, going through the day before they arrived.

Down there in town they had probably told the story of his meeting with the sheriff, of his coping with Ducrow and the others. The majority liked him, and this would tell them he could handle himself. Molina and Perrin stood between him and leadership of the gang.

Molina, Perrin, and himself. He shook his head, trying to clear it. Did he want to be an outlaw?

Blowing out the light, he opened the door and stepped out into the night. For a moment he stood listening. It was very quiet. Distant music came from the saloon. He walked down the path toward the town, hoping to see no one, simply to walk and to think. There was no more time. He must decide. Yet how could he leave Ben?

Avoiding the main street of the little settlement, which was composed of a saloon, a store, and a livery stable, as well as a boardinghouse and what was called a hotel but was actually just a big cabin with bunks, he walked down one of the lanes toward the creek.

Several cabins were scattered along the lane, with corrals, stables, and a well or two. He was passing the last cabin before reaching the trees along the small creek when he overheard ". . . at Red Wall."

Abruptly, he stopped. The cabin door was open and light streamed out, but he was in the darkness out of sight.

Kerb Perrin was speaking. "It's a cinch! We'll do it on our own without anybody's say-so. There's about two thousand head of cattle on their range, but there must be at least five hundred head gathered for a drive, and I've got a buyer for them. We'll hit the place about sunup."

"Who's on the place?"

"Only four hands now. If we wait a few days there will be a dozen. They'll be expectin' nothing."

"How many men will we have?"

"A dozen, maybe less. Keep the divvy small. Hell, that Ragan ranch is easy! The boss won't even hear about it until it's too late to stop us. Anyway, he'll never know it was us."

"I wouldn't want him to," Fernandez said.

"To hell with him!" Ducrow said. "All I want is a crack at that Bastian kid!"

"Stick with me," Perrin said, "and I'll set him up for you."

"You said there were some women?" Ducrow suggested.

"Two white girls are visiting there, and there's two Mexican maids and the mother of the girls. I want the younger girl. What happens to the others is none of my business."

Fernandez looked uneasy. "It is not good," he said. "The women, I mean. Steal cattle, yes. But women? They will hunt you forever."

Perrin shrugged. "Who will be left to talk?"

Ducrow glanced at him, wetting his lips. Fernandez said nothing. After a bit he muttered, "Killing a man is one thing."

"You want to be left out?" Perrin demanded. "You don't have to go."

"I'll go."

"What happens if Ben Curry finds out? He doesn't miss much, you know."

"What happens? If he opens his mouth I'll kill him." There was a pause, then he added, "I never wanted to kill anybody the way I've wanted to kill him. He thinks he's the big man! I'll show him who's top dog!"

"What about Bastian?"

Perrin waved a dismissing hand. "He's your prob-lem! If you an' Fernandez can't figure a way to han-dle him, then you aren't the men I think you are."

"He's quick," Ducrow remarked. "It won't do to think he's easy."

"You handle him."

"And you handle Ben Curry?" The voice was that of the man named Bayless. "He may not be young anymore, but he's hell on wheels with a gun."

"Forget him! You three, along with Clatt, Panell, Monson, and Kiefer, will go with us. Nine out of ten will be with us in makin' the break. There's been a lot of dissatisfaction lately. The boys don't like bein' tied down so much. Sure, they've got money, but what good does it do them?"

"Molina wants to raid the Mormons," Bayless commented. "They've a lot of fat stock and some damn good horses."

Mike Bastian waited no longer. The chance of dis-covery was too great. His first thought was to go at once to Ben Curry, but he might betray his interest in Drusilla and the time was not ripe for that.

What would Ben Curry say if he learned the foster son he had raised to be an outlaw was in love with his daughter? A foster son who had nothing, and no prospects?

Yet what could he do?

Ben Curry would know the girls and their mother were at Red Wall, and he would be going to see them. If he kept an eye on Ben he might find Ben's shortcut to the V-Bar.

Recalling other times when Ben had left, Mike knew the route had to be much quicker than any he could guess at. It was probably further west and south, possibly some way across the Grand Canyon, although knowing the enormous depth of the canyon he could not picture a possible route.

He would have to wait. He wanted to see Drusilla again but now he must wait here, watch Perrin, and do what he could to protect Ben.

How fast was Ben now? And how tough? Speed of draw was the least consideration. Nerve and a steady hand were infinitely more important.

If there was as much unrest in the gang as Perrin implied, something might break loose at any moment. He had known the outlaws were restless. Most of them had become outlaws to avoid discipline. Ben had commanded them longer than anyone would have believed, their loyalty due in part to the returns, in part to the carefully prepared escapes, as well as fear of his far-reaching power. Now there was fear that he was losing his grip.

Mike felt a sudden urge to saddle his horse and ride away forever, to escape all the cruelty, conniving, and hatred that lay dormant here. He could ride now by way of the Kaibab Trail through the forest. Living as he did, it might be a week before they even knew he was gone.

Yet to run now, no matter how much he wished to be away, would be to give up all hope of seeing Dru again. Moreover, whatever future he chose he could not abandon Ben in his hour of need.

Returning to his room he sat down on his bed to

think. Roundy first and then Doc Sawyer, each seemed to be hoping he would give it up and get out before it was too late. Doc said it was his life, but was it?

There was a light tap at the door. Gun in hand, he reached for the latch. Roundy stepped in, glancing at the gun.

"Gettin' jumpy, Mike? I don't blame you."

Mike explained what he had heard. Roundy heard him out and then asked, "Mike? Have you heard of Dave Lenaker?"

"You mean that Colorado gunman?"

"He's headed this way. Ben Curry just got word that he's coming out to take over the gang."

"I thought he was one of Ben's best men?"

"So did we all, and so he has been, but more than likely he's afraid Perrin will climb into the saddle, and they have never liked each other."

"Does Ben know?"

"You bet he does! He's mighty wrought up, too. He'd planned on bein' away a few days on one of those trips to Red Wall. Now he can't go."

Doc came in and the three talked, trying to foresee what might happen and what the best strategy would be. Perrin was hot for a break.

"Roundy," Mike suggested, "either me, you, or Doc had better be here at all times, but you two had best sift around and get some of the men on whom we can depend, like Garlin and Colley. Don't get any you have doubts about. Have them drift up this way and be ready for trouble."

"Garlin's with the horse herd," Roundy said, "no way to reach him today without riding down there."

"All right, get him when you can."

When Roundy had gone, Mike went out to the porch overlooking the canyon. The night was dark, although the stars were bright and there were no clouds.

Somehow he must warn them at the V-Bar, but whom could he trust? The secret of the ranch and its people was not his, but Ben's. Nobody in the canyon would carry any message in any way harmful to another member of the gang. He could get a dozen men by using Ben's name, but that was just what he dared not do.

Ben knew how to get over there in a hurry, but how? And how could he find out in time?

The date for the raid on the treasure train was the twentieth, and there had been talk of a raid into eastern Colorado. Was that to be the twentieth also?

Dave Lenaker was on his way here. If Ben knew that, Perrin might know also. Such things were hard to keep secret, especially when there seemed no reason for keeping them secret.

For a long time he lay awake, trying to think his way to a solution. He must talk to Ben Curry. He must warn him and tell him what he knew.

His window was open and he could hear the far-off howling of coyotes. He found himself wishing he was out there in his wilderness, away from all this, walking down one of those long, long valleys or climbing among the aspen, up to timberline, where the spruce ended and the tundra began. Up to the sliderock slopes where the springs were born.

There was freedom there, and peace, and there was no worry about such men as Kerb Perrin.

He sat up suddenly. He was not cut out for an outlaw, and he had known it all the time. He had played with the idea because it was what was expected of him, but now he knew it was not for him. Yet much as he wished to just ride away from it all, there was no way it could be done. No matter what he was to other men, Ben Curry had been a father to him, gruff but kindly, his affection only shown through a friendly squeeze on the shoulder or, when he was younger, a casual cuff and a ruffling of his hair.

Now Ben's back was to the wall, his lovely daughters and wife in danger and nobody to help but him.

Of course there was Roundy and there was Doc and a few loyal men, but nobody who could stand up to Molina or Perrin or Lenaker, if it came to that. There was only him, and this was what he had been raised for.

He lay down again, staring wide-eyed into the darkness. He would need all his training, all his skill. Perrin was a wily, dangerous man, good with a gun, but cunning as well. And he would know Ben Curry because he would have studied him all those years.

Tomorrow, he told himself. I've got to move tomorrow, and I must talk to Ben. I must make him see what is happening and how he must tell me how to reach his family in a hurry.

His eyes opened again. This was the end. He could

see it clearly now. Ben Curry had held them together but he could do so no longer, nor could anybody else, no matter how well trained.

Many of them were good men who just got started off down the wrong track, but others were murderers and thieves, and the wild animals were about to turn on their keeper.

Tomorrow . . . tomorrow he would see what could be done.

Tomorrow. . . .

CHAPTER 9

THE RED WALL RANCH, also called the V-Bar, lay at the head of a small canyon, an isolated oasis at the upper end of a network of small canyons watered by scattered springs and runoff from the cliffs.

It was such a place as only an Indian, an outlaw on the run, or a wandering prospector might find. During a wet year the range would support cattle, but in a dry year much of it was semidesert, offering little.

Ben Curry had found the place a dozen years before and had with the help of some Indian friends put up a stone house, stable, and corrals. He had piped water into the house from a spring, had kept some cedars growing close by, and had planted a few other trees, carefully watered until their roots were down.

By handling cattle judiciously, taking advantage of the wet years and cutting the numbers during dry periods, a man might do well with a small ranching operation. Ben Curry did not intend to live out his life there, simply to maintain it as a secret base of operations. Doc Sawyer knew of the place, but only Roundy had actually been there.

The ranch house was a low building almost lost to view against the cliffs some distance behind, and partly screened by trees. A man might easily ride by the lower end of the canyon without even seeing the house, which was on a low knoll. Behind it and between the house and the canyon wall were the corrals, a stable, a storage shed, and a smokehouse.

"It's so alone!" Juliana said, looking down the long narrow valley. "I love it here, but it scares me, too!"

Drusilla said nothing, but she, too, was looking down the long valley. It was beautiful, it was remote, it was wild and strange. Maybe that was why she loved it so much, and maybe that was why she so looked forward to coming back, even though the visit would be a short one.

"I often wonder why Papa chose such an out-of-the-way place," Juliana went on. "He could have a ranch anywhere. I don't believe anyone lives within a hundred miles of us."

"We aren't that far from Flagstaff. It just seems far."

"But what if something went wrong?"

"We'd have to fend for ourselves," Dru said. "That's why you should learn to shoot. Someday you may have to."

"There was trouble in town after we left," Juliana said. "I heard the men talking about it. Some sort of a fight."

"I wish Papa would come."

It was very quiet. From the steps before the bunkhouse where the men slept they heard the low mur-

mur of voices. It was a comfortable sound. Night was
falling and already they had a light on out there.

"It gives me the shivers."

"There's nothing to be afraid of. There are four
men out there."

They were silent, and Juliana drew the shades.
Walking back to the table Dru took the chimney from
the lamp, struck a match, and touched it to the wick.
Replacing the lamp globe she drew back a chair. "It's
almost time for supper."

"I don't like it, Dru. I don't feel right. Something's
going to happen."

Dru looked at her sister, a cool, appraising glance.
Juliana had these feelings once in a while, and they
were often right. It was foolish to be afraid. Still—

By day anyone approaching could be seen for
some distance, but at night?

"I'll speak to the men," she said, "after supper."

Juliana left the room and Dru walked slowly back
to the window. Standing at one side she could still see
far down the valley, but in a few minutes it would be
too dark.

Now she was feeling it, too. Suddenly she turned
and went to her room. From her duffel she took a
derringer her father had given her, and checked it.

Loaded, and both barrels. She slipped it into her
skirt pocket.

It *was* lonely! Where was Pa? He had warned
them not to expect him at any particular time but
that he would come. They could depend on that.

Of late Drusilla had been doing some wondering
of her own. Several times her father had met them at

the ranch, but it was not until the last time that she
had noticed anything strange. The first thing was his
horse. Pa said he had come far, but his horse did not
look it or act it. Thinking back she remembered that
his horses had never seemed hard ridden, yet if Pa
came from somewhere near, where could it be?

There was nothing near. There was only wilderness.

She looked down the valley again. Now all was
darkness, with only a few stars hanging in the sky.

Supper was a quiet meal. None of them felt like
talking very much, but then her mother had never
been much of a talker.

"How did you meet Papa?" Dru asked suddenly.

"Papa? Oh—?" Her mother hesitated, then
laughed. "It was at a party, back in Texas. Some riders stopped by, and of course, everybody was welcome in those days, so we invited them to join us.

"We danced, talked a little, and finally ate supper
together. Two of the men who came with him stayed
with their horses, although once in a while one of the
others would change places so they could come in
and enjoy the party, too.

"He was so *big*! And so very good looking! He
wasn't from anywhere around there, and when I
asked him he said he was from Colorado but he had
been back farther east to buy cattle.

"They left before daylight but he was back a week
later, but that time he was alone. He stayed several
days and we went driving and riding, and something
about him kind of scared the others away. There
were several young men who—"

"Courted you?"

"You could call it that. But after he came they were all frightened away."

"He frightened them? What did he do?"

"Oh, nothing, really. There was just something about him. He was very romantic, you know. So mysterious! He would come, stay around a while, then be gone."

"He is still mysterious," Dru said quietly.

Her mother glanced up quickly, defensively. "Not really. His work just keeps him away. I have always understood that."

When supper was over, Dru went out back. The door of the bunkhouse was open, and Voyle Ragan was coming toward her.

"Uncle Voyle? When will Papa be here?"

"I don't know, honey. He can't always get here when he wants. What's the trouble?"

"Juliana is scared. I don't know why, but she is. She says something's wrong, and when she feels that way she is usually right."

He was a tall, lean man. He managed the ranch, talked little, but was a kindly, thoughtful man.

"Nothing to worry about," he said. "Not many folks even know about this place. We don't see many strangers."

She was silent. If she were to ask, would he tell her? "Uncle Voyle—?" She hesitated. "What does Papa *really* do?"

She watched him turn his head and glance down the canyon, then he said quietly, "Why, you know as well as I do. He buys cattle, drives 'em sometimes, sells 'em to the best buyer. He does right well, but it keeps him on the road."

He spoke hastily, before she could interrupt. "He never talks business at home. It just ain't his way. Buyin' like he does he goes out to ranches, deals with some pretty rough men, time to time. Sometimes he buys an' sells cows without ever movin' 'em. Knows the buyer before he buys. He's a shrewd man."

"I believe he is. I believe you are, too, Uncle Voyle, and that story will satisfy Mama and Juliana but not me. I want to know where Papa is, and I want to know why he always comes from over toward the canyon."

"Where'd you get that idea?"

"I've seen him. Once when I was riding I saw him coming up through the draw. And when he gets here after those long rides his horses are always so fresh."

Voyle Ragan was disturbed. For years he had been afraid of this. Juliana would accept things as they seemed to be, but not Drusilla. She was like her father, and missed nothing.

"Have you talked to anybody else about this?"

"Who would I talk to? I've seen no one."

"Well, don't. Not even the men here. Your papa knows what he's about, but you leave it lay. The less you know the better, and the fewer questions you ask the fewer other folks are apt to ask."

"So that's it." Her voice fell. "He's an outlaw, isn't he?"

"Well—"

"I've suspected it for a long time, but somehow he never seemed the type."

"No, Dru, he surely doesn't. That's just it, he never did. Your ma, well, I think she *knows* but she'd not mention it, and she'd not admit it, even to herself.

"He'll be along soon, and when he does you get him alone if you're of a mind to, and ask him, hisself. But not where anybody can hear you."

"Uncle Voyle? I don't believe he'll come tonight. I think there has been trouble. Call it intuition, whatever you wish. I have a feeling."

Her uncle shifted his feet. "Now, don't you be gettin' scared," he said. "There's nothing—"

"Yes, there is." She paused. "Uncle Voyle, when we were coming up from Flagstaff, we were followed."

"Followed?" He was startled.

"By a man who came out of a draw from the east. He kept back out of sight most of the time, like he did not wish to be seen, but he was following us. Just before we came into Red Wall he disappeared."

Voyle Ragan was worried. The fact that Ben Curry owned the V-Bar was a well-kept secret, and Voyle knew Ben had prevented any raiding of ranches close to the hideout in Toadstool Canyon. His argument had been simple. Leave the nearby ranches alone and they would be friendly in time of need. Yet Voyle had never trusted Curry's leadership. Sooner or later some of the outlaws would break loose and go to raiding on their own.

Who would be scouting the place? The law? There was none within miles, and no breath of suspicion invited their interest.

Outlaws? What would be more likely, with cattle already gathered and ready for moving?

"Don't scare your sister or your mother with this, Dru. You can use your rifle, so keep it handy. I'll have a talk with the boys." He paused. "Just where did you see that rider?"

He listened to her description, recognizing the area at once. "Tomorrow I'll have a look," he told her.

"You be careful," she said. Then she changed the subject. "Uncle Voyle? Did you ever hear of a cowboy named Mike Bastian?"

Voyle Ragan was glad of the darkness. "Can't say I have," he said cautiously. "What about him?"

"We met him on the way up here. In fact, it was he who helped us get a rig to bring us in after we left the stage."

"Most any western man would have helped you."

"I know, but it was he who helped, and—there was something about him—"

"I'll bet I know," Voyle said, amused. "He was probably young and good looking."

She laughed. "He was that, too, but it was the way he moved. Like a big cat. But like somebody else, too. I can't think who he reminded me of, but somebody I know very well."

"Mike Bastian? I'll remember the name. He tell you what he did?"

"No. No, I don't believe he did. I thought he might be a cowboy, or even a hunter. He was wearing buckskins. You know, like the Indians do." She paused again, then trying to keep her tone casual she said, "He asked if he could come calling."

Voyle Ragan chuckled. "And I'll bet you said yes."

It was her turn to laugh. "Of course. Could I be less than hospitable? After all, this is the West!"

After she had gone inside Voyle Ragan walked to the bunkhouse. Two of the hands were already asleep or pretending to be. The other had one boot off and one on. "You," Voyle said to him, "put that other boot back on. You're taking the first watch."

"Watch? For what?"

"Somebody followed that buckboard when it brought the womenfolks. I don't like it."

One of the other men, Garfield, sat up. "Been meanin' to tell you, Voyle. I come on some hoss tracks up on the rim a few days back. Looked like somebody had been scoutin' us."

"All right, you boys all know your business. Make like it's Injun times again, only these Injuns will be white men and outlaws, more than likely.

"We're bunchin' cows for a drive. In a few days we'll have a dozen more hands on the place. I'd guess they know that, so if anything happens it will be before the other hands get here.

"Don't any of you get more than two, three miles from the place. Watch your back trails, and if anything happens you hightail it back here to stand by the womenfolks."

"Hell, I never knowed any outlaw to bother women!" Garfield protested.

"I know, but we're away out in the hills. Mighty

few folks even know we're here, an' there's outlaws an' outlaws."

Garfield pulled on his other boot and straightened up, hitching his suspenders over his shoulders. Then he slung on his gun-belt.

"Take your Winchester, too, you may need it."

Garfield gave him a bleak look. One of the hands started to snore, and Voyle indicated him. "Wake him up at midnight. He can stay on watch until three, and then Pete can take over until daybreak."

Voyle Ragan went outside and stopped, listening. It was quiet, very quiet. He walked up to the house and to his room. After he had hung his gun-belt to the headboard of his bed, he placed his Winchester across the washstand, close by.

It had been a long time since he had been in a shooting fight and he wasn't sure he was up to it.

CHAPTER 10

MORNING WAS COOL and clear, yet Mike Bastian could feel disaster in the air. Dressing hurriedly, he headed for the boardinghouse. Only a few men were eating, and there was no talk among them. They glanced up when he entered, but only one nodded briefly. Mike was finishing his coffee when Kerb Perrin entered.

Instantly, Mike was on guard. Perrin walked with an arrogance that was unusual with him. He glanced at Mike Bastian, then seated himself and began to eat.

Roundy came in, then Doc Sawyer. That meant that Ben Curry was alone in the stone house. A moment later Ducrow entered, followed by Kiefer, then by Rocky Clatt, Monson, and Panell.

His cup halfway to his mouth Mike remembered suddenly that these were the men Perrin planned to use in the raid on the Ragan ranch. That could mean the raid was to happen today!

He looked up to see Roundy push back from the table, his coffee unfinished. The old woodsman hurried outside and disappeared.

Mike put down his own cup and stood up. Instantly, he was motionless. The hard prod of a gun was in his back and a voice was saying, "Don't move!"

The voice was that of Fernandez. Perrin was leaning back in his chair, smiling.

"Sorry to surprise you, Bastian," Perrin said, "but with Lenaker on the way here we had to move fast. By the time he arrives I'll be in the saddle. Some of the boys wanted to kill you but I figure you'd be a bargaining point with the old man.

"He might be a hard kernel to dig out of that stone shell of his, but with you for an argument I think we can make him listen."

"You're mistaken," Mike said quietly. "He doesn't care what happens to me. He can afford to be rid of me and recruit somebody else. He won't let you get away with it."

"I shall, though. You see, Rigger Molina left this morning with ten of his boys to knock over the gold train."

"That was to be my job," Mike said.

"I swapped with him. He could have the gold train if he left me the bank job. I must admit"—Perrin smiled—"that I neglected to tell him about the twelve armed guards, and the number who had shotguns. In fact, I told him only three guards would be along. I believe that will take care of him for me."

Perrin turned abruptly. "Take his gun and tie his hands behind his back, then shove him into the street. I want the old man to see him."

"What about him?" Kiefer pointed a gun at Doc.

"Leave him alone. We may need a doctor, and he knows where his bread is buttered."

Mike Bastian was coldly, bitterly angry with himself. He should have been more careful! His attention had been on Perrin, and Fernandez had slipped up behind him. He was shoved into the street. The morning sun was warming things up and he was pushed out in its full glare, facing up the street toward the stone house.

He felt a fierce triumph. No matter what happened to him the old man would be tough to move out of that house. The sun was full in his face as it would be in the faces of any attackers, and the old man would be up there, ready, with a high-powered rifle. From the doors and windows he could command the whole settlement.

Perrin had moved out behind a wall of logs and sandbags hastily thrown up in the street. "Come on down, Curry!" he shouted. "Come down with your hands up or we'll kill your son!"

There was no reply, no evidence they had been heard.

"I'm not his son," Bastian said. "We're not even kin. He raised me to do a job, and he can get along without me. He doesn't give a tinker's damn about me."

"He hasn't heard you," Clatt said. "Let's just rush the place."

"You rush it," Kiefer said. "I'll just set back an' watch!"

Despite his helplessness, Mike felt a glow of satisfaction. Ben Curry was a wily fighter. He knew that once he responded, their threat would have force. It was useless to kill Bastian unless Curry could see it, useless to waste him when they did not know Ben was even listening.

Perrin had been positive Curry would come out rather than sacrifice Mike, and now they were not even sure their message was reaching him. Nor, Mike knew, were they sure Curry would give himself up to save him. At first, it had seemed logical. Now he knew Perrin was no longer sure. Nor were those who followed him.

"Come on out!" Perrin shouted. "We'll give you an' Bastian each a horse and a mile's start. Otherwise you both die! We've got dynamite!"

"Perrin," Mike said, "you've played the fool. Curry doesn't care whether I live or die. He won't come out, and there's no way to get him out. Don't you think the old man has planned for this? When did you ever know him not to plan for everything?"

Mike was talking as much for the effect on Perrin's men as for Perrin himself. If he could make them doubt his leadership, they might, out of fear of Ben Curry, turn on Perrin.

Perrin ignored him. Some of the men stirred restlessly, and one or two looked around as if wondering if someone was creeping up on them. Ben Curry was a shrewd fighter. Suppose he had planned for this? What would he have done?

"All he has to do, Kerb," Mike said, "is wait for Dave Lenaker to show. Then he can make a deal with Dave, and where will you be? Out in the cold with these men who were crazy enough to listen to you!"

"Shut up!" Perrin's tone was angry. "He'll come out, all right. He's just stallin'!"

"Let's open fire on the place!" Ducrow was impatient. "Or rush it, like Clatt suggested!"

"Hell!" Kiefer was disgusted. "Why bother? Let's take all we can get away with an' leave! There's the cattle, at least two hundred head of the best ridin' stock in the country, and what all. Rigger's gone. Lenaker ain't here yet. We've got a clear field."

"Take pennies when there's millions up in that stone house?" Kerb's veins swelled with anger. "There's the loot of years up in that house! A strong room with gold in it, stacks of money! With all that to be had you'd run off with a few head of cows?"

Kiefer was silent but unconvinced.

"There is no strong room," Mike told them. "I sleep in one room, Doc Sawyer in another, and there's one for the old man. The only thing he's got stored up there is ammunition. He's got enough ammunition to fight a war, and he's got the range of every place in town. Any time he's good an' ready he can start takin' you out, one at a time."

Standing in the bright sunlight of the dusty street, Mike looked toward the stone house. All the love and loyalty he felt for the old man up there came back with a rush. Whatever he was, good or bad, he owed Ben Curry. Perhaps Curry had reared him for a life of crime, but to Ben Curry it had not been a bad life. He lived like a feudal lord and had no respect for any law he did not make himself.

Wrong though he might be he had taken the orphan boy Mike Bastian and given him a start. He

could never, Mike now realized, have become an outlaw. It was not in him to steal, rob, and kill. That did
not mean he could not be loyal now to the man who
had reared him and given him a home when he had
none.

He was fiercely proud of that old man up there
alone. Like a cornered grizzly, he would fight to the
death. He, Mike Bastian, might die here in the street,
but he hoped only that Ben Curry would stay in his
stone shell and defeat them all.

Kerb Perrin was stumped. He had planned quickly
when he heard Lenaker was on his way to Toadstool
Canyon. When Lenaker arrived he would have men
with him, and the fight for control could turn into an
ugly three- or four-way battle.

With Molina out of the way he had been sure he
would take over from Curry and be ready for Dave
Lenaker when he arrived. He would be waiting in
ambush for Lenaker and his men. They would never
live to enter the canyon. Now, suddenly, both his
planning and his timing had gone awry.

The idea that Ben Curry would not even reply had
not occurred to him. That he might not surrender,
Perrin had foreseen, and he had a sniper posted to
pick him off if he so much as showed himself.

"If you boys want to make a strike"—Mike spoke
casually—"there's that bank in eastern Colorado.
According to all we hear it is ripe and waiting to be
taken."

Nobody said anything but he knew they would be
thinking. He doubted if any of them really wanted to

face Ben Curry. He might be old, but how old was he? And how tough?

There was simply nothing he could do. At any moment Perrin might decide to kill him where he stood. Out in the open as he was, hands tied behind him, there was nothing he could do but think.

What had become of Roundy? The old trapper had risen suddenly and left the table, and Roundy had left his coffee unfinished, an almost unheard-of move for Roundy. Could he be in league with Perrin? No, that was impossible. Roundy had always been Ben Curry's friend and had never liked Kerb Perrin.

Yet where was he? Up there with Ben? That was likely, yet Roundy had a dislike of being cooped up. He liked to range free. He was a moving fighter, not given to defense unless forced to it. Wherever he was he would be doing what was necessary, of that Mike was sure.

"All right," Perrin said suddenly, "there's no use all of us watchin' one old man." He glanced at Bastian. "That was a good idea of yours, about that bank. We'll just hold you, knock off that Ragan place, and then the old man will be ready to quit. We'll take care of him an' ride east an' pick off the bank."

Bastian was led back from the street. His ankles were tied and he was thrown into a dark room in the rear of the store.

His thoughts were in a turmoil, and he fought to bring them to order. If he was to get out of this alive he must *think*. There was always a way if one but tried.

If Perrin's men rode to the Red Wall they would find only four hands on the V-Bar. They would strike suddenly, and they knew how to do what must be done. Juliana, Dru, and their mother would be helpless. Four men, five counting Voyle Ragan, could not stand against a surprise attack.

And here he was bound hand and foot.

Desperately, he fought the ropes that bound him, but those who did the tying were skilled with ropes and had tied many a head of cattle and horses.

As his eyes became accustomed to the darkness he looked for something he could use to free himself, but there was nothing. No projecting corner, no nail, nothing.

Outside all was still. Had they gone? He had no way of knowing, but if Perrin was not gone he soon would be, leaving enough men to watch Ben Curry. Mike ceased struggling and tried to think. If he could get free and discover Ben's secret route across the river he might beat Perrin to it and be waiting when the outlaws arrived.

Where was Roundy? And Doc Sawyer?

Just when he had all but given up a solution came to him so simple that he cursed himself for a fool. Mike rolled over to his knees. Fortunately he was wearing boots instead of the moccasins he often wore in the woods. Bracing one spur against another to keep them from turning, he began to chafe the rawhide against the rowel of the spur. He wore big-roweled Mexican spurs, given him by Sawyer, spurs with many sawlike teeth instead of long spikes.

Desperately, he sawed until his muscles ached and

he was streaming with perspiration. Once, pausing to rest, he heard a rattle of hoofs from outside. Several horses being ridden away.

Were they just going? He might have a chance, if only—

Boots sounded on the floor. Someone was coming! And just when he was cutting through the rawhide! Fearful they would guess what he was doing, he rolled to his side.

The door opened. It was Snake Fernandez. In one hand he held a knife. The other shoulder was still bandaged from Bastian's bullet.

"You shoot Fernandez, eh? Now we see! I am Yaqui! I know many ways to make a man bleed! I shall cut you into pieces. I shall cut slowly, very slowly. You will see!"

Bastian lay on his shoulder, staring at the half-breed. Stooping over him, the Yaqui pricked him with the knife point, but Bastian did not move.

Enraged, Fernandez tossed up the knife and caught it in his fist. "You do not jump, eh? I make you jump!"

Viciously, he stabbed down, and Mike, braced for the stab, turned to his back and kicked out with both feet. The heels of his boots caught Fernandez on the knees and knocked him over backwards. As he fell, Mike rolled to his knees and jerked hard at the raw-hide binding his wrists.

Something snapped, and Mike pulled and strained.

Fernandez was on his feet, recovering his fallen knife.

Fighting the ropes that tied him, Bastian threw

himself at Fernandez's legs, but the Yaqui leaped back, turning to face him with knife in hand. Bastian turned himself, keeping his feet toward the other man, then as the outlaw moved in, Mike lifted his bound feet and slashed downward.

His spurs caught the outlaw on the inside of the thigh, slashing down, ripping his striped pant leg and cutting a deep gash in his leg.

Fernandez staggered, cursing, and Bastian jerked hard on his bound wrists and felt something give. The rawhide ropes started to fall away, and shaking them loose he whirled himself around and grabbed at the outlaw's ankle, jerking it toward him.

Fernandez came down with a crash, but fighting like an injured wildcat, he attempted to break free. Mike, grasping Fernandez's wrist with one hand, took his throat with the other, shutting down with all the strength developed from years of training for just such trouble.

Struggling, the man tried to break free, but Mike's grip was too strong. Fernandez's face went dark with blood. He struggled, thrashed, and his struggles grew weaker. Releasing his grip on the man's throat, Bastian slugged him viciously on the chin, then hit him again.

Taking the knife from the unconscious man's hand, Mike cut his ankles free and stood up, chafing his wrists to get the circulation back.

Now—!

CHAPTER 11

A MOMENT, HE HESITATED. Looking down at the unconscious man. Fernandez was wearing no gun but usually had one. It could have been left outside the door. Careful to make no sound, as he had no idea what awaited, he moved to the door and opened it cautiously.

The street before him was deserted. His hands felt awkward from their long constraint and he worked his fingers continually. He pushed the door wider and stepped into it. The first thing he saw was Fernandez's gun-belt hanging over the back of a chair.

He had taken two steps toward it when a man stepped out of the bunkhouse. The fellow had a toothpick in his hand and was just putting it to his mouth when he saw Mike Bastian. Letting out a yelp of surprise he dropped the toothpick and went for his gun.

It was scarcely fifteen feet and Mike threw the knife underhanded, pitching it point first off the palm of his hand. It flashed in the sun as the gun lifted. The man grunted and dropped his gun, reaching for the hilt of the knife buried in his stomach, his features twisted with shock.

Mike grabbed Fernandez's gun-belt and slung it on, one gun-butt forward, the other back. Then he ran for the boardinghouse where his own guns had been taken from him. He sprang through the door, then froze.

Doc Sawyer was there with a shotgun in his hands. Four of Perrin's men were backed against the wall. "I've been waiting for you," Doc said. "I didn't want to kill these men but wasn't about to try tying them up."

Mike's gun-belt was on the table. He stripped off Fernandez's guns and belted on his own, then thrust both of Fernandez's guns into his waistband.

"Down on the floor!" he ordered them. "On your faces!"

It was the work of minutes to hogtie all four. He gathered their weapons.

"Where's Roundy?"

"I haven't seen him since he walked out of the boardinghouse. He just stepped out and disappeared. I've been wondering."

"Forget him. Let's go up to the house and get Ben Curry, then we can figure this out. We don't have much time. They're headed for the V-Bar."

Doc looked sick. "I didn't know. My lord! And those womenfolks—!"

Together they went out the back door and walked along the line of buildings. Mike carried his hat in his hand, the easier to be recognized. He knew that Ben could see them, and he wanted to be recognized.

Sawyer was excited but trying to be calm. He had seen many gun battles but had never been directly involved in one.

Side by side, gambling against a shot from the stone house or someone of the Perrin outfit they had not rounded up, they mounted the stone stairs to the house.

There was no sound from within. Opening the door they stepped into the living room and looked around. There was no sign of life. On the floor was a box of rifle cartridges scattered over the carpet.

A muffled cry reached them, and Mike paused, listening. Then he ran out of the room and up the staircase to the fortress room. He stopped abruptly. Sawyer was only a step behind him.

This was the room no outsider had seen, not even Doc. A thick-walled stone room with water trickling into it from a stone pipe, falling into a trough and then out through a hole in the bottom of a large stone basin. The supply of water could not be cut off, and there was a supply of food stored in the room.

The door was heavy and could be locked from within. Nothing short of dynamite could blast a way into this room.

This was Ben Curry's last resort, but he lay on the floor now, his face twisted with pain. "Broke m' leg! Tried to move too fast an' I'm too heavy!

"Slipped on the steps, dragged m'self up here." He looked up at Mike. "Good for you, son! I was afraid they'd killed you. Got away by yourself, did you?"

"Yes, Pa."

Ben looked at him, then away.

Sawyer had dropped to his knees, examining the older man's leg. "This is a bad break, Ben. We won't be able to move you very far."

"Get me a mattress to lay on where I can see out of the window. You an' me, Mike. We'll handle 'em!"

"I can't stay, Pa. I've got to go."

Ben Curry's face turned gray with shock. He stared, unbelieving. "Boy, I never thought—"

"You don't understand, Pa. I know where Perrin's gone. He's off to raid the V-Bar. He wants the cattle and the women. He figured he could get you any time."

The old man lunged with a wild effort to get up, but Doc pushed him back. Before he could speak, Mike explained what had happened, then added, "You've got to tell me how you cross the Colorado. With luck I can beat them to the ranch."

Ben Curry relaxed slowly. He was himself again, and despite the pain Mike knew he was feeling, Curry's brain was working. "You could do it, but it will take some riding. They're well on their way by now, and Kerb will know where to get fresh horses. He won't waste time."

He leaned back, accepting the bottle Sawyer brought to him. "I never was much on this stuff, but right now—" He took a long drink, then eased his position a little. Quickly but coolly, he outlined the trip that lay ahead. "You can do it," he added, "but that's a narrow, dangerous trail. The first time we went over it we lost a man and two horses.

"Once you get to the river you'll find an old Navajo. Been a friend of mine for years. He keeps some horses for me and watches the trail. Once across the river you get a horse from him. He knows about you."

Mike got to his feet and picked up some added ammunition. "Make him comfortable, Doc. Do all you can."

"What about Dave Lenaker?" Doc protested.

"I'll handle Lenaker!" Curry flared. "I may have a busted leg but I can still handle a gun. You get a splint on the leg and rig me some kind of a crutch. I'll take it from there!"

He paused. "I'm going to kill him when he shows in that street, but if something happens and you have to do it, Mike, don't hesitate. If you kill either Perrin or Ducrow you'd be doing the West a favor. I've been thinkin' of it for years.

"But remember this about Lenaker. If I miss out somehow or you see him first, *watch his left hand*!"

Mike went down the steps to his own room and picked up his .44 Winchester rifle. It was the work of a minute to throw a saddle on a horse. Ben Curry and Doc could hold out for weeks in that room if need be, but the risk was dynamite thrown through or against the window. He would have to ride to the Red Wall and get back as quickly as possible.

Mike Bastian rode from the stable on the dappled gray and turned into a winding trail that led down through the ponderosa and the aspen to the hidden trail leading to the canyon. He had never ridden this trail, although he had discovered it once by accident. The gray was in fine fettle, and he let it have its head. They moved swiftly, weaving through the woods, crossing a meadow or two, and twice fording the same stream.

As he rode he tried to picture where Perrin would be at this time. He knew nothing of the secret crossing, of course, and must ride the long way around. Even with fresh horses and getting little sleep it would take time. His own ride would cover less than a quarter of the distance but was steeper and rougher. Nor could Mike even imagine how he would cross the river. All Ben had told him was there was a crossing and he would see when he got there.

"It'll take nerve, boy! *Nerve!* But remember, I've done it a dozen times, and I'm a bigger man than you!"

This was all new country to him, for he was heading southwest into the wild, unknown region toward the canyon of the Colorado, a region he had never traversed. It was unknown country to everyone but Ben Curry, the Indians, and perhaps some itinerant trapper.

Occasionally the trail broke out of the trees and let him have a tremendous view of broken canyons and soaring towers of rock.

He must ride fast and keep going. He was sorry now that he had not picked up some jerky before leaving Ben, for there would be nothing to eat until he reached the ranch, and then there might not be time.

Once, atop a long rise, he drew up to let the gray catch its wind and sat the saddle, looking out across the country. In the purple distance he could see the gaping maw of the great canyon. He spat into the dust, feeling a chill. How could any lone man hope to cross *that*?

And at the end of the ride, if he made it, there would be Kerb Perrin.

He had seen Perrin shoot. The man was fast with a gun and deadly. He was almost too fast.

Patches of snow still showed themselves around the roots of trees or on the shaded slopes. He dismounted, letting the gray drink from a clear, cold mountain stream that cascaded down a steep slope, disappearing into the brush, then appearing once more. Beaver had built a dam, formed a wide pool, and built a house at the pond's edge. He drank well above the pond and let the gray rest for a few minutes while he stood, listening to the silence and watching a beaver push through the water with a green branch which it would bury in the bottom of the pond against the days when snow fell and the pond was covered with ice.

He walked back to the gray and, putting a toe in the stirrup, swung to the saddle. "All right, boy, we've got a way to go."

The gray trotted down a narrow path covered with pine needles, then suddenly out of the ponderosa and into an eyebrow of trail that clung hopefully to a cliff's sheer face. One stirrup scraped the wall, the other hung in space. The drop was a thousand feet or more to the first steep slope, and if one slid off that it was another thousand to the bottom. The gray was a good mountain horse who went where only the imagination should go, and picked its way with care until the trail dipped into the forest again.

Shadows fell across the trail, and he glimpsed a white rock he had been told to watch for. He turned sharply left and went down through a steep cleft of sliderock where his horse simply braced its legs and slid to emerge at the foot of the mesa with a long, rolling plain before him.

A whiskey-jack flew up, flying ahead to light in a tree he must pass. It knew where men were there was often food, and it followed along, perhaps as much for the companionship as for whatever he might leave. "No time, old boy," he said. "I've a long way to go while the sun's still up."

He was tired, and he knew the gray was slowing down, but that meant nothing now.

Would he arrive in time? What was it like there? If he did not arrive in time, what then? There was a coldness in him at the thought, something he had never known before, but he knew what he would have to do. He would hunt them down, every man of them, no matter how long it took or how far the trail led. He would find them.

Mike rode down through heaped-up rocks, which had been falling for ages down upon this slope, rolling into position and lying there. Here the trail dipped and wound, and he thought of what lay ahead.

He had never been in a gunfight. He had drawn and fired at Fernandez without thinking, but he knew he had been lucky. In a gun battle you were shooting at living men who could fire back, and would. How would he react when hit by flying lead? He must face that, make up his mind, once and for all. If he got hit he must take it and fire back.

He had known men who had done it. He had known men hit several times who kept on shooting. Cole Younger at Northfield had been hit eleven times and escaped to finally survive and go to prison. His brothers had each been hit several times yet had survived, at least for the time. If they had done it, he could do it.

Perrin and Ducrow, those two he must kill, for they were the worst. If they fell the others might pull out. No matter what, he must kill them. He could not die trying. He had it to do.

Suddenly the forest seemed to split open and he was on the edge of that vast blue immensity that was the canyon. He drew the gray to a stand, gasping in wonder. Even the weary horse pricked its ears. Here and there through the misty blue and purple of distance red islands of stone loomed up, their tops crested with the gold of the last light.

The gray horse was beaten and weary now and Mike turned the horse down another of those cliff-hanging trails that hung above a vast gorge, and the gray stumbled on, seeming to know its day was almost done.

Dozing in the saddle, Mike Bastian felt the horse come to a halt. He could feel dampness rising from the canyon and heard the subdued roar of rapids as the river plunged through the narrow walls. In front of him was a square of light.

"Hello, the house!" he called out. He stepped down from the saddle as the door opened.

"Who's there?"

"Mike Bastian!" He walked toward the house, rifle in hand. "Riding for Ben Curry!"

The man backed into the house. He was an old Navajo but his eyes were bright and sharp. He took in Mike at a glance.

"I'll need a horse. I'm crossing the river tonight."

The old Indian chuckled. "It cannot be done. You cannot cross the river tonight."

"There'll be a moon. When it rises, I'll go across."

The Navajo shrugged. "You eat. You need eat first."

"There are horses?"

The chuckle again. "If you wish a horse you find him on other side. My brother is there. He has horses, the very best horses.

"Eat," he said, "then rest. When the moon rises, I will speak." He paused. "Nobody ever try to cross at night. It is impossible, I think."

Mike Bastian listened to the water. No man could swim that, nor any horse, nor could a boat cross it. He said as much, and the old Indian chuckled again. "If you cross," he said, "you cross on a wire."

"A *wire*?"

"Sleep now. You need sleep. You will see."

A wire? Mike shook his head. That was impossible. It was ridiculous. The old man was joking.

He crossed to the bunk and lay down, staring up into firelit darkness, and the sound of the rushing waters filled the night, and then he slept.

And in his dreams a red-eyed man came at him, guns blazing. . . .

CHAPTER 12

BORDEN CHANTRY GLANCED out the kitchen window toward the train station. When the tracks were built through town they fortunately passed within fifty yards of his home, so he could drink coffee, eat his breakfast or supper, and watch people get on and off the trains. Not that very many ever did. Four days out of five the train just whistled and went on through.

He liked seeing the trains come in, and so did Bess. She brought coffee to the table now, and with it the old subject. "I wish you would give it serious thought, Borden. This is no place to raise a boy."

"I grew up in the West," he replied mildly.

"That's different. You enjoy this life, but I want something different for Tom. I want him to go to school back East. I want him to have a fine education. I don't want him to grow up riding after cows or wearing a gun."

He glanced toward the station again. He knew how she felt, but what could he do back East? She just didn't understand. He had always been somebody wherever he was, but that was because all he knew was the West. Back East the best he could do would be to manage a livery stable or do common labor. He was a fair hand at blacksmithing but not at the kind of work he would have to do back East.

Right now he was holding down two jobs and getting paid for them both. He was sheriff of the county and marshal of the town, and for the first time in years he was saving money. If he could work a couple of years more he could buy cows and go back to ranching. All he had now was about sixty head running on open range and about thirty head of horses, five of which did not belong to him, but ran with his stock.

"I have thought about it, Bess. How would I make a living back there? All I know is cattle and range country. I got my start hunting buffalo and went to cow punching and then ranching. Drouth and a tough banker broke me, and these folks were kind enough to give me a job as town marshal."

"You'd find something, Borden. I know you would. I just don't want Tom growing up out here. All he does is run with that orphan McCoy boy, and he thinks about nothing but guns and horses."

"Billy's a good boy," Borden said. "Ever since he lost his pa a few years ago he's been batching. You should see that cabin. Keeps it spotless. That's a good lad, and he will do well."

"At what?"

He shifted uncomfortably. This discussion occurred at least once a week, and Bess was living a dream. She wanted to go back where she'd come from, wanted Tom to grow up as her brothers had, as her father had. What she wasn't realizing was that they would be poor. You could be poor in the West and if you worked nobody paid much attention, but back East you fell into a different class. There were things you were left out of, places you weren't invited. At least, that was the way he heard it. He had only been east twice, for a few days each time.

The first was when he took Bess east after they were married. He saw at a glance the money he was earning out west wouldn't take them far in the East. If he could just get started ranching again . . . well, he knew he could make it. Right now, for example, the range was good. What he needed was three to five hundred head. With that kind of a start and a break on the weather he could soon build himself a herd.

Back East? He would be a poor relation, and that was all.

"You just wait, Bess. I'll get back to ranching again. I've been thinking about those cows of Hyatt Johnson's. He's going to sell out, and I could pick them up if I had a little cash. Maybe—"

"Borden? Why did Mr. Sackett come over here to see you? Is there trouble?"

He sipped his coffee. "No, not really. Just something we're interested in. Maybe it's a fool idea, Bess, but you recall those letters I had? The one I wrote to Fort Worth? And El Paso?

"Well, Sackett thinks the same as I do. He believes most of those robberies were pulled off by one big outfit, with one man in charge."

"What kind of a man would it take to keep that many outlaws in line?"

Of course, that was it. Bess, as usual, had put her finger on it. The kind of man needed to ramrod that sort of operation wouldn't be any average sort of man, he would be something special, and he would have been noticed, and if noticed, remembered.

Between them Sackett and he had now come up with eighteen jobs in which the robberies were pulled off with quick, neat work—nobody shot, nobody caught, no trail left. Men appeared, pulled off the robbery, and disappeared.

Usually one or more of the men loafed around town beforehand, studying the bank, getting the layout. No strangers had been spotted that could not be accounted for.

Yet a few days ago he'd had an idea and had written to Sackett. Whoever was ramrodding that gang had been keeping his men under cover, so how about checking up on known outlaws who hadn't been showing themselves and were not in prison?

It had been his experience that they couldn't stay under cover for long. They showed up in another robbery, got into a saloon brawl, something of the kind. Most of them were the sort who craved attention, and it was unlike them to stay out of sight for long.

His thoughts returned to the kind of man to control such an operation, and suddenly, he had a hunch.

Bess, who had come up with the key question in the Joe Sackett murder when she asked how he got to town, had done it again. *What kind of a man would it take to keep such men in line?* Or words to that effect.

And he knew. At least, he had a hunch. That big man who had left the horses with him, the big man who might have been a big cattleman or something. He might not be the man but he was the kind of man who could do it. If anybody could.

Borden Chantry pulled out his watch, glancing at it. Barely nine o'clock. Mary Ann would be up even if the rest of her girls were sleeping. Bess wouldn't like it but he would have to see Mary Ann, and it was best to tell her first. Somebody else certainly would mention it if he was seen going to her house. Police business occasionally called him there, and she had been a help in that murder case. Moreover, Mary Ann had been around. There was little she did not know about outlaws.

He emptied his cup and got to his feet, reaching for his hat. "Bess, I've got to see Mary Ann."

Her face stiffened. "Is that necessary?"

"Bess, you just gave me a lead when you spoke about the kind of man it would take. You're right, as always. Remember how your question opened up that murder case? I think you've done it again."

"Then why see Mary Ann?"

"That woman knows more outlaws than anybody in the country, and she's on the grapevine. Whatever is going on, she knows."

"But will she tell you?"

"Bess, this is her town, too. She has money in that bank."

Mary Ann was in the kitchen drinking coffee when he rapped on the door. "Come in," she said, "but keep your voice down. The girls worked late last night."

He accepted the coffee she offered. Mary Ann was no longer young but she was still a beautiful woman, and during her rare appearances on the street she dressed sedately and conducted herself modestly. She was a shrewd, intelligent woman who listened as he laid it out for her.

"What I want to know," he said, "is who the boss man is, or the name of any other outlaw who has dropped from sight."

He paused. "And it is just possible that boss man stopped overnight here in town five or six years back. Maybe less."

She gathered her kimono a little tighter. "What's happening?"

"I think, among other things, the local bank. It's just a hunch, but Tyrel Sackett thinks so, too."

"I've money in that bank. Most of my savings."

Chantry waited, letting her think. Most of the outlaws were known to girls such as these, and the girls moved around a good bit and talked among themselves. There was not much they did not know.

"Rigger Molina," she said.

"I don't know him."

"Not the boss. He hasn't brains enough, but he's big, tough, and very, very good with a gun."

"And . . . ?"

"Nobody has seen anything of him for two or three years. That's unlike him. The girls were talking of it the other day with some fellow who was in here. Molina isn't the sort of man you can miss.

"He's big, powerful, thick arms and legs, shock of hair, broad jaw, small eyes, moves like a cat, and he swaggers. He doesn't brag, doesn't have to, you can look at him and you know he's got it. The point is that he is not a man to remain unnoticed. If he had been around he would have been seen, talked about."

"Odd that I don't know him."

"No, it isn't. Not really. He's out of Vernal, up in Utah. He worked in Montana, the Dakotas, and Idaho. He killed a man in Catlow Valley, up in Oregon. Some dispute over a steer. When they came after him he killed two more and wounded the sheriff. He loaded the sheriff on his horse and took him to a doctor, banged on the door, and left him.

"The thing was, Molina rode ten miles out of his way to get help for that sheriff. He could have let him die."

She got up. "Wait . . . I'll get Daphne. She's the new girl."

Daphne was a tall, slinky blonde who looked from the badge on Chantry's vest to his face. "How'd a good-lookin' man like you start to wearin' that thing?"

"Lay off, Daph. He's married, and happily."

"All the good ones are." She sat down and lit a cigarette. "You want to know about the Rigger? He's a good badman, sheriff."

"Where is he?"

She drew on her cigarette. "This guy really a friend of yours, Mary Ann?"

"Yes, he is. He will be a friend of yours, too, if you level with him."

She waited, dusted ash from her cigarette, and said, "The Rigger was nothing to me but he was to a girlfriend of mine. They saw each other reg'lar. Then one day he told her to take care of herself, he'd be out of circulation for a while, but when he came back he'd be loaded.

"We hear that sort of talk all the time, but not from Molina. He never had to brag.

"He said he was tying up with an outfit that would make it big, and then he went away. One of the girls I ran into said she saw him eating in a restaurant in Pioche with some tall, thin galoot."

She paused. "I hope this isn't trouble for him. He was an all right guy. Didn't have an enemy in the world unless it was Kerb Perrin."

"I hope he kills him," Mary Ann said. "Perrin beat up one of my girls once, when I was working in Goldfield. He beat her up and he liked doing it."

She paused. "Come to think of it, I haven't heard anything of him for a long time, either."

Borden Chantry walked back to the office, mulling it over in his mind. He might have something.

Kim Baca, his own deputy, had been a skilled horse thief at one time, and he knew everybody on what some called the owl-hoot trail. He had never heard it called that himself.

An hour later he knew much more. Kim Baca knew both Molina and Perrin, liked Molina, didn't like Perrin. Both had dropped from sight. So had Colley, the Deadwood outlaw. When Baca thought about it, there were a dozen or more he could name who simply hadn't been around.

Chantry was having his supper and watching the train when he remembered the big man who had left the horses with him. He should have asked Mary Ann about him. Thinking about it, he remembered detecting a change in her face when he spoke of the man stopping over in town a few years back. She had sort of tightened her kimono, and he knew Mary Ann, somewhat. It was a gesture she made when she had an idea or made a decision.

What did she know?

He wished Sackett was here. And it took too long for a letter—

What was he thinking of? The telegraph! Why couldn't he get used to the idea of the telegraph? Ever since they put the railroad in it had been here, available.

He walked through the twilight to the station and wrote out his message.

Rigger Molina—Kerb Perrin—Colley.
Big man, middleaged or older. Six three,
two forty. Strong face, big hands. Deep scar
below right earlobe.

Sitting beside the fire that night Borden Chantry drew a long breath and waited, and then he spoke quietly. "Bess? If you're set on it, I mean if you want it that much, we could try it back East."

She stopped sewing and lowered her hands to her lap. "I haven't wanted it because this is my world, but for you—for you I'd do it." He hesitated again.

"One reason I haven't wanted to go is that I don't want you to see me a failure.

"I've been enough of one so far." He waved a hand around. "They like me here. I was a good marshal, I guess, so they elected me sheriff. I didn't make it ranching because of the weather. Maybe I wouldn't have made it, anyway. I don't know what I'd do back East where nobody knows me and where I've no skills they can use.

"The thing is, I want you to be happy, and you've thought about little else these past few years. When my term's up, we'll go."

"Borden, I—I don't know what to say. I do want to go back. You can't realize how much I've hated all this. The shooting, the killing—"

"That could happen anywhere." He brought his knee up and pulled off a boot. "This thing I'm into, the thing I'm helping Sackett with. We've got to finish that first."

He pulled off the other boot and got up. "I'm going to bed, Bess. I'm a little tired. You an' Tom make your plans. I'll go with you."

He carried his boots into the bedroom and put them down. Then he took off his gun-belt and hung it on the back of the chair that stood beside his sleeping place. Taking off his vest he sat down.

He was being a damned fool. What *could* he do back East?

Bess wanted to live in town. She was remembering how it had been for her father, who had kept a store or something. He couldn't keep a store, and he had too little education to compete. He would be—

There was a rap at the door. He stood up, reaching for his gun-belt. He listened, heard Bess replying to something, then the door closed.

She came into the room with a sheet of paper in her hand. "It was the telegrapher. He was going home but he brought this over, thinking it might be important."

It was from Tyrel Sackett, and it was just two words: *Ben Curry*.

CHAPTER 13

HE KNEW THE NAME.
Borden Chantry was at his battered office desk when Kim Baca came in. Chantry glanced up at his young deputy. Baca had been one of the most skillful horse thieves in the country before he became Chantry's deputy, and he knew the men who rode the outlaw trail and their ways.

"Kim? What do you know about Ben Curry?"

"Leave him alone."

Chantry shuffled some papers on his desk. "I may have some horses of his. If I am not mistaken he left some at the ranch a while back."

"If he did he will pick them up in his own good time. Leave him alone, Chief. He's trouble, big trouble."

"When he picks those horses up he will be on the run. We want him, Baca."

Kim ran his fingers through his dark hair. "If the horses are here they are here for a purpose. Ben Curry doesn't make many mistakes, and he doesn't make any false moves."

"I think he wants our bank," Chantry commented mildly.

"He won't do it himself, and my suggestion is stay out of the way and let him have it. You aren't gettin' paid to get killed."

"I'm paid to do a job, Kim. So are you."

"Yeah, I know." Baca paused. "I'm told you could pick up an easy thousand dollars by bein' out of town for a few days. You're sheriff, too. You could be investigatin' that counterfeit money that's been showin' up."

"Kim, you can tell whoever passed that word along that I'm not for sale. An officer who turns crooked is worse than any thief. A thief is out to steal and is at least honest in his intentions. A police officer takes an oath to support the law." Chantry pushed back from his desk. "If I was a judge and a crooked officer came up before me, I'd give him the stiffest sentence the law permitted."

Kim shrugged. "I figured you'd think thataway but I was told to pass the word along."

"Let them know that I'll be here," Chantry said, "and I'll be ready."

"It won't be Ben Curry," Kim said. "More than likely it will be Molina or Perrin or somebody new. There's a word out that Ben's got a new man, specially trained for the work."

"Do you have friends in that outfit?"

Baca hesitated, then shrugged. "No, I can't say I do. I never ran with a gang, you know. Worked alone. I know some of those boys, and there's good men among 'em or they wouldn't have stayed together so long. The word is that the old man is lettin' go, and the boys are restless."

"Thanks, and if you hear anything, let me know."

Baca shook his head. "Since I pinned on this badge I don't hear as much. However," he added, "I could put it in my pocket and ride over to Denver. Down along Larimer Street I might hear something."

"Do that. Here." Chantry held out a couple of gold coins. "I'm not carrying very much but use that. Let me know what you hear."

He paused. "Kim, Tyrel Sackett is workin' with me on this. I think there's going to be a lot goin' on this spring. Something can happen wherever there's a gold shipment, a payroll, or a bank that looks easy.

"They've been quiet all winter, so I think they'll be lookin' for a big one."

Kim Baca walked outside. Well, now! A ride to Denver, all expenses paid and some money to spend!

There were few secrets. Somebody always talked, and somebody always listened. Most of the western outlaws were known, and when they traveled they were noticed. No matter what their orders were there was always one who wanted to see an old girlfriend or stop off for a drink with old acquaintances.

For not the first time he was glad he was no longer a wanted man. He could see what was happening. Chantry and Sackett were comparing notes, and if they were, others would be, and then the law would start to close in.

He would have to be very, very careful. Ben Curry, or so the word was, wanted no killings during the commission of a holdup, but that was a matter of policy, and he would and had killed when pursued.

His own knowledge of Ben Curry's operation was limited to a comment here and there or a rumor. He had not thought about a pattern to the crimes until Chantry pointed it out, showing his series of clippings, reward posters, and notifications from other peace officers. There *was* a pattern, and a pattern meant a trail one could follow, and not all trails were tracks on the ground. Behavior patterns were difficult to eliminate, and in moments of stress one reverted to them.

The outlaw might believe he was winning for a time, but someone—like Chantry or Sackett— somebody was carefully working out the trail.

His weakness had always been horses, better horses than he could afford to buy. He loved them for their speed, their beauty, and just for themselves. He had stolen some of the finest horses in the West, but the trouble was such horses were usually known. Just a few weeks ago Chantry had taken him out to Chantry's old ranch and pointed out a handsome bay gelding.

Kim caught his breath when he saw the horse. It was a beauty.

"The man who owned that horse," Chantry said, "I sent to prison. He'll do twenty years if he lasts that long, and as he's a sick man now neither of us believes he will. I asked him what to do with his gear.

" 'Keep my guns, rope, and saddle,' he told me. 'I never sold my saddle and never will.'

" 'What about the gelding?' I asked.

" 'That's the finest horse I ever rode, and I wouldn't want him in the wrong hands,' he told me."

Chantry said, "I knew how he felt, and I told him I had a man who loved horses and would care for him as long as he lived. He asked me who, and I told him 'Kim Baca.' "

"He laughed, Kim, laughed real hard. 'Kim? Well, I'll be damned! Sure, I'll write a bill of sale for him. I'll bet that's the first bill of sale Kim ever had, and I'll bet it was the first horse he was ever given!' "

"You mean he gave that horse to me?"

"He surely did. Here's the bill of sale. And Kim?"

"Yes, sir?"

"When you ride that horse, carry the bill of sale with you. Anytime the law sees you on a fine horse they are apt to ask questions."

Kim had caught up the gelding and saddled it. Across the pasture, bunched together like they were old friends, were five other horses, all of them fine stock.

"That them?" he asked, knowing the answer.

"That's them, just waiting to be picked up when somebody is traveling fast and needs fresh horses to outdistance a posse."

He turned as Chantry followed him outside. They rode out of town together.

"Take me a few days to get to Denver," Kim suggested.

"Take the steam cars. They'll put your horse in a stock car, or if there isn't one, I'll get him in the baggage car."

"Why didn't I think of that? I can't get used to

thinking of trains and railroads and such." He turned his horse away. "See you in about a week."

Borden Chantry sat his horse, watching Kim ride away. The sky was clear and blue, the air fresh and cool with morning. From the low hill on which he sat his horse he could see the distant Spanish Peaks far off to the westward. Some day he'd ride over that way again, a beautiful country. Closer, he saw a coyote trotting across the distance, stalking some antelope.

The coyote was wasting his time unless there was an old one or a cripple amongst them. No fawns yet that he had seen, but several of the antelope looked about ready, which was probably why the coyotes were closing in, waiting until the does were down and helpless.

No wolf or coyote could catch an antelope running, and several times he had seen antelope run right away from the fastest greyhounds and stag hounds.

He looked around slowly, drinking in the vast distances. Bess wanted him to leave this. He loved her, but could he do it? And she did not realize what a position she was putting before him. She had always seen him in a position of strength, as a rancher and then as a town marshal and sheriff. Back East he would have none of the needed skills, nor had he the education required there.

He started his horse and walked it slowly down the slope. Kim Baca was, of course, right. He should be paying more attention to counterfeiting. For years now it had been one of the major crimes in the West, and a comparatively safe one. A bogus bill might be months or even years in reaching a bank where it

could be identified, and a lot of queer money had
been showing up. Both he and Baca believed the
source was close by.

First, he must prepare for an attempted robbery.
The Ben Curry boys had refrained from killing, but he
knew that if capture appeared to be a possibility, they
would fight. He was going to alert the town and select
a couple of deputies for the emergency. If Ben Curry
wanted his bank he would have to get it the hard way.

This new man Baca mentioned? What about him?
Who would he be?

Whoever it was, they could expect a shooting
fight, and with the kind of men Ben Curry recruited
that meant somebody would get killed.

Unless he could figure out a way, a plan.

He didn't want to kill anyone or see anyone be
killed, but the choice might not be his.

AT THE RED WALL it was quiet. A few cows grazed
on the meadows below the house. Dru Ragan stood
on the wide porch and looked broodingly down the
canyon. There had been nothing friendly about that
rider she had seen. Nor was he an Indian. An Indian
might not have approached the house and out of curiosity might just have looked it over, but it had been
a white man and had he been friendly he would have
come on up to the ranch for a meal or at least for coffee.

Most of her life had been spent in the East, but she
was instinctively western in her thinking. From first
sight she had loved all this wild, lonely, wonderful

country with its marvelous red canyons, its blue distance, its green forests, and the golden leaves of the aspen when autumn came to the hills. She loved seeing the cattle out there, and riding through the sage on horseback, topping out on a high ridge with magnificent views in every direction.

This had long been sacred land to the Indians, and the great peaks they revered had become important to her, also.

Now there was this other thing, this lurking danger. Or was it danger?

Riding around she scouted the country, knowing little about tracking but looking for the obvious. She came upon the tracks of the rider she had seen, and followed them. Several times, from several positions, he had looked at the ranch. That was obvious enough, for she could see where he had stopped and his horse had moved restlessly, leaving many tracks in the one position.

She wanted to follow the tracks, as they seemed plain enough, but the hour was late. She glanced off to the north where the great canyon lay. Someday she wanted to see it. Someday she would stand on its rim.

Voyle Ragan was waiting when she rode up. He was standing on the porch where she had looked over the country before beginning her ride.

He was worried, she could see that. "See anything?"

"Tracks," she said. "Somebody has definitely been looking us over."

With its shielding canyon walls darkness came early to the V-Bar. The Red Walls lost their color to shadows, and the night lay like velvet upon the meadows and the range. Only the stars were bright, and the windows of the house and the bunkhouse.

They would need to keep watch again. Voyle walked back into the house and took his rifle from the rack. He would keep it at hand. He should put on a belt gun but hesitated because of the women and as he rarely wore one around the house.

He had never thought of the night as an enemy. Now he was no longer sure.

Ben had a means of crossing the canyon. How, he could not imagine, but it worried him that others might discover that route. Ben's success had been due to keeping it a secret and to the fact that no one suspected he had a reason for crossing.

He blew out the lamp in the living room, returning to the kitchen where the girls and their mother were already seated for supper.

The night was very still. He sat down, and there was little talk where usually there was much, only a pleasant rattle of dishes and an occasional low-voiced request for something. Voyle kept his ears sharp for the slightest sound from outside.

Why couldn't all this have waited until the roundup and trail-drive hands were here?

That was why it was happening now. Or was he just worrying too much? Maybe that cowhand who was looking them over was just shy. He had known them to be. Maybe there was nothing to worry about at all.

———

A SOFT WIND blew down the ranges, whispering in the pines, stirring the leaves of the aspen. Out on the open country beyond the canyon an antelope twitched its ears, listening.

A sound whispered across the stillness, a far-off sound as of something moving. The antelope listened as the sound faded, and then it rested again.

A cloud blotted out the moon, the wind stirred again, and a tumbleweed rolled a short distance and stopped as the wind eased. Overhead a bat swooped and dived and searched for insects in the night.

At the V-Bar the women had gone to bed. Voyle Ragan blew out the last lamp and walked to the porch to listen. The night was still.

Walking back through the house he went down the back steps and crossed to the bunkhouse. Garfield was sitting outside.

"Better get out in front of the house or on the porch," he suggested. "You can hear better."

Garfield got up. Taking his rifle he walked around to the front steps. This was kind of silly. What was Voyle afraid of, anyway? He put the rifle down and lit his pipe.

He looked at the stars. Mighty pretty. A man out in this country looked at the stars a lot. The trouble was a man was so busy he forgot to take time to enjoy.

Garfield did not know he was looking at the stars for the last time. He did not know that within a matter of hours he would be dead, sprawled on the ground, cold and dead.

CHAPTER 14

Mike Bastian awakened with a start. For a few minutes he lay still, trying to remember where he was and why he was there.

He sat up. His guns were there, and his rifle. He was in a small stone house and he could hear the river. He was supposed to cross that river, although from the sound he could not imagine anyone crossing it. The old Indian was seated by the fireplace, smoking. He glanced over at Mike.

"You had better eat something. The moon is rising." He paused. "Not even he ever tried to cross at night."

"You speak very good English," Mike commented, thinking his own was none too good.

The Indian gestured with his pipe. "I was guide for a missionary when small. He was a kind, sincere man, trying to teach Indians something they already knew better than he, although the words were different."

"He taught you to speak well, anyway."

"He did. I spoke English with him every day for six years. He taught me something about healing, and I think my mother taught him something about it. She was very wise about herbs.

"He asked me one time why I never went to church, and I told him that I went to the mountains. I told him my church was a mountainside somewhere to watch the day pass and the clouds. I told him, 'I will go to your church if you will come to mine.' I think by the time he left us he liked mine better."

The old Indian turned to Mike. "When you are tired and the world is too much with you, go to the mountains and sit, or to some place alone. Even a church is better when it is empty. So it is that I think, but who am I? I am an old Navajo who talks too much because he wishes to speak his English."

When Mike had eaten they walked together to a trail that led them up even higher and then to a place where there was a ledge. "Ben Curry needed two years to build this bridge," the Indian said, "and nobody has crossed it but him, and only a few times."

Mike stared into the roaring darkness with consternation. Cross there? Nothing could. No man could even stay afloat in such water, nor could any boat live except, with luck, riding the current downstream. The river was narrow here. At least, it was narrower than elsewhere. The water piled up at the entrance to the chasm and came roaring through with power. Of course, this was spring and snow in the mountains was melting.

"There! You see? There is the bridge. It is a bridge of wire cable made fast to rings in the rock."

He stared across the black canyon where two thin threads were scarcely visible, two threads of steel that lost themselves in the blackness across the canyon, one thread some five feet above the other. On the bare cold rock he stood and stared and felt fear, real fear for the first time.

"You mean . . . Ben Curry crossed *that*?"

"Several times."

"Have you crossed it?"

The old Navajo shrugged. "The other side is no different than here. If there is anything over there I want I shall ride around by Lee's Ferry or the Crossing of the Fathers. I have too little time to hurry."

A faint mist arose from the tumbling waters below. Mike Bastian looked at the two wires and his mind said *No!* He wet his lips with his tongue, lips gone suddenly dry. Yet, Ben Curry had done it.

How far was it across there? How long would it take?

He was deep in the canyon, deep in this vast cleft cutting to the red heart of the earth. Around him were rocks once bare to the world's winds, rocks that had been earth, pounded by rain, swept by hail, crushed down by eons of time's changing. Looking up he could glimpse a few stars, looking out across the deep he could see nothing but looming blackness. Somewhere, somehow, the cables were made fast, and if they were strong enough to hold Ben Curry, who was forty pounds heavier, they would be strong enough for him.

He put his rifle over his head and across one shoulder. Again he hesitated, but there was no other way. Kerb Perrin was riding to the V-Bar. He must be there before Perrin arrived. Taking hold of the upper cable he put a tentative foot on the lower and eased himself out. A moment passed, then he glanced back. The old Navajo was gone.

A slow wind whispered along the canyon walls, stirring the night with ghostly murmurings, then was lost down the blackness of the canyon. Mike Bastian took a deep breath. He had never liked heights and was glad the depths below were lost in darkness except where white water showed around the rocks, catching the few last rays of light.

He edged out. It was not too late. He could go back. He could return for his horse and ride back to Toadstool Canyon, but what of Drusilla and Juliana? What of their mother? And the cowboys . . . would they be warned? Would they have any idea until death swept down upon them?

He edged out further, clinging to the upper strand, not lifting his feet above the cable but sliding them. One slip and he would be gone.

How far to the water? Two hundred feet? More like five hundred, although he was already deep in the canyon. He remembered now, hearing some talk of this when he was a small boy and it was being done. Roundy it had been, he told Ben of finding an iron ring in the wall, wondering why it was there. No doubt the idea had come from that.

He tried to keep his mind away from the awful depth below, and the roaring waters of the spring floods. Many times he had seen the river when it was like this, although never from this point. He moved on. At places the wire was damp from mist thrown up from the raging waters. Once he slipped, his foot touching some mud left from the boot of a previous traveler. His foot shot from under him and he was saved only by his tight grip on the wire. Slowly, carefully, he pulled himself erect once more, feeling for the cable with his foot.

Now he was at the lowest point above the river, and from now on he would be climbing a little, pushing his foot along the slanting cable. Carefully, he worked himself along. He could see the loom of the cliff on the opposite side.

Was there a good place to get off? Would the rock be wet and slippery? He remembered climbing out of a cliff dwelling once when the ladder stopped below the top of the boulder against which it rested, a smooth, polished boulder, and he had to work himself to the edge, turn himself around, and clinging to that polished surface, feel for the steps of the ladder with a five-hundred-foot drop behind him. He had not liked it then, and would not now.

Little by little he edged along until he was under the loom of the cliff, and he was trembling when he stepped off the cable into the safety of a rocky cavern at the cable's end. He was so relieved to be safely across that he did not immediately notice the Indian who sat awaiting him.

The Navajo got up and without a word led him along a trail to a cabin built in a branch canyon. Tethered at the door of the cabin was a huge bay stallion. With a wave for the Indian, Mike stepped into the saddle and was off, the stallion taking the trail it obviously knew.

Would Perrin travel by night? Bastian doubted it. After all, what was the reason for hurry? His victims awaited him, practically helpless, and with no warning of what impended. The trail led steadily upward. No doubt Curry himself had ridden this horse. It obviously knew where it was going, and he was eager to be there.

As the trail widened the horse broke into a swinging lope that ate up the ground.

The country was rugged, red rock, cedar, and occasional flats where the purple sage grew, only not purple tonight, merely dark patches here and there. As for the cedar, he could smell it, and the pinyons, too.

Dawn came slowly, breaking through long streaks of gray cloud. He drew up at a pool of snow water and drank, then let the stallion drink. He took a strip of jerky from his small pack and chewed on it while he unslung his rifle and edged it into the boot.

His approach must be with great care. He was not sure as to the exact position of the ranch, and Perrin might already be there. As he drew nearer he must ride slower to make the beat of his horse's hoofs less loud.

He knew the men he was facing, and they were skilled and dangerous fighting men.

The shadows were almost gone, but the sun was not yet up. Mike slowed the stallion to a walk although the animal tugged at the bit, eager to go.

Now he must listen, listen for any sound, a movement, a distant shot—

———

DRUSILLA RAGAN BRUSHED her hair thoughtfully, then pinned it up. She could hear her mother moving in the next room, and the Mexican girls who cared for the house were tidying up.

Juliana was outside talking to the young blond cowboy who had been hired to gentle some horses.

Suddenly Drusilla heard Juliana's footsteps. She came into the door, cheeks glowing. "Aren't you ready? I'm famished!"

"I'll be along." Then as Juliana turned away, she asked, "What did you think of him, Julie? That cowboy or whatever he was who got the buckboard for us? Wasn't he the best-looking thing you ever saw?"

"Oh? You mean Mike Bastian? I was wondering why you were mooning around in here. Usually you're the first one up. Yes, I expect he is good looking. And you know something? He reminded me of Pa. Oh, not in looks, but some of his mannerisms."

Drusilla was no sooner seated at breakfast than she decided to ask Uncle Voyle about Mike Bastian again.

Ragan knew the girls had met Mike Bastian in Weaver, and he knew about the gold train, so he tried to keep his expression bland. "Did you say his name was Bastian? I don't place it. You said he was wearing buckskins? Sounds more like a hunter than a cowboy, but you can never tell."

"He's probably a hunter from up in the Kaibab. It's unlikely you will see him again. It's pretty wild up there on the other side of the canyon."

"The driver of the buckboard said there were out-laws up there," Juliana said.

"It could be. It is very wild up there," and he added truthfully, "I've never been up there."

He lifted his head, listening for a moment. He thought he had heard horses coming, but it was too soon for Ben to arrive. If anyone else stopped by he would have to get rid of them, and promptly. Visi-tors, however, were extremely rare.

Then he heard the sound again, closer. He got up quickly. "Stay here!" He spoke more sharply than intended.

His immediate fear was a posse, and then he rec-ognized Kerb Perrin. He had seen Perrin many times, but doubted if Perrin had ever seen him or had any idea who he was. There were several riders, and they were Ben's men, but Ben had always assured him the outlaws knew nothing of the V-Bar or his connection to it.

He walked out on the porch. "How are you?" He spoke mildly, suddenly aware that he was not even wearing a gun. "Anything I can do for you?"

Where were his hands? Why had the sentry not warned him?

"You can make as little trouble as possible," Kerb Perrin said harshly. "You can stay out of the way and maybe you won't get hurt. We heard there were women here. We want them and we want your cat-tle."

Voyle Ragan stood tall and alone. "My advice is for you to ride out of here, and ride fast. You aren't welcome."

He paused, stalling for time. "The only women here are decent women, who are visitors."

Ducrow slid from his horse and shucked his Winchester. At that moment Garfield appeared at the corner of the corral. "All right!" he shouted. "Back off there!"

The others were on the ground, spreading out. Garfield was cool. He stepped out, his rifle up. "Back off, I said!"

He saw a movement and his eyes flickered and Ducrow shot across the saddle. Garfield took the bullet and fired back. A man beyond Ducrow spun and fell, Garfield worked the lever on his rifle and Ducrow shot into him. The cowhand backed up, going to his knees, fighting to get his rifle up. Another shot knocked him over, yet he still struggled.

Ignoring the shooting, Kerb Perrin started up the steps and Voyle Ragan hit him in the mouth. The blow was sudden, unexpected, and it landed flush. Perrin put his hand to his mouth and brought it away, bloody.

"For that, I shall kill you!"

"Not yet, Perrin!"

The voice had the ring of challenge, and Kerb knew it at once. He was shocked. Bastian *here*?

He had left Bastian a prisoner at Toadstool Canyon, so how could he be here, of all places? And if he was free that meant Ben Curry was back in the saddle.

He must kill Mike Bastian and kill him now!

"You're making fools of yourselves! Ben Curry is not through and this place is under his protection!

He sent me to stop you. All those who get in the saddle and ride out of here now will be in the clear. If you don't want to fight Ben Curry get going, and get going *now*!"

Kerb Perrin went for his gun.

CHAPTER 15

KERB PERRIN KNEW he was going to kill Mike Bastian.

There had never been a time when he was not sure of his skill with a gun, and now even more so. Who did this kid think he was, anyway?

Kerb Perrin was smiling as his hand dropped to his gun, yet even as his gun cleared its holster he saw a stab of flame from the muzzle of Bastian's gun and something slugged him hard in the midsection.

Staggered and perplexed, he took a step backward. Whatever hit him had knocked his gun out of line, and the shot he fired went into the dirt out in front of him. He lifted his gun to swing it into line when something hit him again, half turning him.

What was wrong? He struggled with his gun, which was suddenly very heavy. There was a strange feeling in his stomach, something never experienced before. Suddenly he was on his knees and could not remember how he got there. A dark pool was forming near his knees, and he must have slipped.

He started to rise. He was to kill Mike Bastian, he had to kill him. He peered across the space between them. Bastian was standing with a gun in his hand, holding his fire. What was the matter with Bastian? Did he think he, Kerb Perrin, needed time? He lunged to his feet and stood swaying. His legs felt numb and he was having a hard time getting his breath.

That blood . . . it was *his* blood! He had been shot. Mike Bastian had beaten him. Beaten *him*? Like hell! His gun muzzle started to lift, then fell from his fingers. He had another gun. He would—

He reached for it and fell into the dust. His eyes opened wide, he tried to scream a protest but no sound came. Kerb Perrin was dead.

In the instant that Kerb Perrin's gun came up too late, Ducrow wheeled and ran into the house. Kiefer, seeing his leader fall, grabbed for his own gun and was killed by a shot from Voyle Ragan's rifle, hurriedly grabbed from its place beside the door.

The others broke and ran for their horses, and Mike got off one quick shot as they fled. He had lifted his gun for a final shot when he heard the scream.

Ducrow had come to the ranch for women, and it was a woman he intended to have. Dashing through the house while all eyes were on the shooting, he was just in time to see Juliana, horrified at the killing, run for her bedroom. The bedroom window was open and Ducrow grabbed her and threw her bodily from the window. Before she could rise he was through the window and had caught her up from the ground. Swiftly, he threw her across the saddle of a horse and with the few swift turns of the experienced hand she was bound hand and foot. Her scream was partly stifled by a back-handed blow across the mouth, then

Ducrow leaped to the saddle of Perrin's mount, which was better than his own. Catching up the bridle of her horse he went out of the yard at a dead run.

Mike had wheeled, running for the house, believing the scream had come from inside. By the time he glimpsed them they were disappearing into the pines. He saw two horses, one rider and—

"Where's Juliana?" he shouted.

He had already glimpsed Drusilla standing on the porch. Voyle Ragan ran around the house. "He's got Julie!" he yelled. "I'll get a horse!"

"You stay here! Take care of the women and the ranch! I'll go after Juliana!"

He walked to his horse, thumbing shells into his gun. Dru Ragan started toward another horse.

"You go back to the house!" he ordered.

"She's my sister!" Dru flared. "When we do find her she may need a woman's care!"

"Come on then, but you'll have to do some riding!"

He wheeled the big bay and was off in a jump. The horse Dru mounted was one of Ben Curry's big horses, bred not only for speed but for staying power.

Mike's mind leaped ahead. Would Ducrow try to return to Toadstool? Or would he join Monson and Clatt? If he did, then Mike was in trouble. He worried about no one of them—but all three?

He held down the bay's pace. He had taken a swift glance at the hoof tracks of the two horses he was trailing.

Mike Bastian went over the situation, trying to view it from Ducrow's standpoint. Ducrow could not know that Juliana was Ben Curry's daughter, but at this stage he probably would not care. Yet he would realize Ben was back in the saddle again, so a return to Toadstool was out of the question. Also, Ducrow would want to keep the girl for himself. That he would kill her had to be understood, for any attack upon a decent woman was sure to end in hanging if he was caught.

Long ago Roundy had taught him that there were more ways to trailing a man than merely following tracks. One must follow the devious trails in a man's mind as well. He tried to think as Ducrow would be thinking.

The fleeing outlaw could not have much, if any, food. On previous forays, however, he must have learned where there was water. Also there were ranch hangouts that he would know. Some of these would be inhabited, others would not. Owing to the maps Ben Curry had him study, Mike knew the locations of all such places.

The trail veered suddenly, turning into the deeper stands of brush, and Mike followed. Drusilla had not spoken since they started, but glancing back he saw her face was dusty and tear streaked, yet he noted with a thrill of satisfaction she had brought her rifle. She *was* Ben Curry's daughter, after all, a fit companion for any man.

He turned his attention to the trail. Ducrow must know he was followed or would be followed, and he would want to leave no trail. Nor was he inexperienced. In his many outlaw raids as one of Ben Curry's men and before he would have had much experience with such things.

And now it had happened. Despite the small lead he had, Ducrow had vanished!

Turning into the thicker desert growth he had dipped down into a sandy wash. There, because of the deep sand and the tracks of cattle and other horses it needed several precious minutes to decide whether he had gone up or down the wash. He searched, trying not to disturb the sand until he had worked it out. Then he saw a recognizable hoofprint following the winding of the wash as it led up-country. Ducrow would not stay in the wash long, as it was tiring for the horses to walk in the deep sand, and he would wish to save his horses' strength.

From there on it was a nightmare. Ducrow rode straight away, then turned at right angles, using every bit of cover he could find and mingling his tracks with others wherever found. At places he had even stopped to brush out tracks, but Roundy's years of training had not been wasted, and Mike clung to the trail like a bloodhound.

Following him, Dru saw him pick up sign where she could see nothing. Once a barely visible track left by the edge of a horseshoe, again a broken twig on a bush they had passed.

Hours passed and the sun began to slide down the western sky. Dru, realizing night would come before they found her sister, was cold with fear for her.

Mike glanced back at her. "You wanted to come," he said, "and I am not stopping because of darkness."

"How can you trail them in the dark?"

"I can't, but I believe I know where they are going and we will have to take a chance."

Darkness closed down upon them. Mike's shirt had stuck to his body with sweat, and now he felt the chill of the night wind, but grimly he rode on. One advantage he had. He had never ridden with the gang, so Ducrow might not suspect he knew of all the hideouts. Ducrow could not know of the hours he had spent with Ben Curry and Roundy going over the trails and checking the hideouts and what he could expect at each one.

The big bay horse seemed unwearied by the miles of travel, yet at times Dru heard Mike speak encouragingly to the big horse. At the edge of a clearing he suddenly drew up, so suddenly she almost rode into him.

"Dru," he whispered, "there's a small ranch ahead. There might be one or more men there, and Ducrow is almost surely there with your sister. I am going to find out."

"I'll come, too."

"Stay here! When I whistle, come and bring the horses. I have skill at this sort of thing, and I have to get close without making a sound."

Removing his boots he slipped on the moccasins he always carried in his saddlebags. He was there a moment, and then he vanished into the darkness, and she heard no sound, nothing. Suddenly a light appeared in a window . . . too soon for him to have reached the cabin.

Moving like a ghost, Mike reached the corral.

There were horses there but it was too dark to make them out. One stood near the bars, and putting a hand out he touched the horse's flank. It was damp with sweat.

Without so much as a whisper of sound, Mike was at the window, his head carefully to one side but peering in.

He saw a square-faced man with a pistol in his hand, and as Mike watched, the man placed the pistol on the table with a towel over it.

Soundless in his moccasins, Mike walked around the house and stepped into the room.

Obviously the man within had been expecting the sound of horse's hoofs or even a jingle of spurs and a sound of boots. Mike's sudden appearance startled him, and he made an almost inadvertent move toward the pistol under the towel.

Bastian closed the door behind him, and the man stared at him. This black-haired young man in buckskins did not look like the law, and he was puzzled but wary.

"You're Walt Sutton. Get your hands away from that table before you get blown wide open! *Move!*"

Sutton backed off hurriedly, and Mike swept the towel off the gun. "If you had tried that I'd have killed you."

"Who are you? What d'you want here?"

"You know damn' well what I want! I am Mike Bastian, Ben Curry's foster son. He owns this ranch. He set you up here, gave you stock to start with! Now you double-cross him. Where's Ducrow?"

Sutton shook his head. "I ain't seen him," he protested.

"You're a liar, Sutton! His horses are in the corral. You're going to tell me where he is or I'll start shooting."

Walt Sutton was unhappy. He knew Ducrow as one of Ben Curry's men who had come for fresh horses. He had never seen this young man before, yet so far as Sutton was aware nobody but Ben Curry and himself knew the facts about the ranch. If this man was lying, how could he know?

"Listen, mister, I don't want no trouble. Least of all with old Ben. He did set me up here, and I been doin' well. Yes, I seen Ducrow, but he told me the law was after him."

"Do I look like the law? Ducrow's kidnapped Voyle Ragan's niece, and they are friends of Ben's. I've got to find him."

"Kidnapped Voyle Ragan's niece? Gosh, mister, I wondered why he wanted two saddle horses."

Mike backed to the door and whistled sharply. "Where did he go?"

"Damned if I know. He rode in here about an hour ago wanting two packhorses with grub and blankets. He took two canteens and then lit out."

Drusilla appeared in the doorway and Sutton's eyes went to her. "I know you," he said. "Evenin', ma'am."

"Get us some grub, and make it quick. Then I want the two best horses Ben left here, and I want them fast!"

Sutton put bread and meat on the table and ducked

out of the door. Mike watched him hurry to the corral and saw him bring two horses from the stable. They were typical Curry horses, big, handsome animals.

Sutton led them to the door and then sacked up some supplies and tied them behind the saddles.

"You've been a help," Mike said, "and I'll tell Ben about it. Now—have you any idea where Ducrow might be going?"

"Well—" Sutton hesitated, obviously frightened. "He'll kill me if he learns I told, but he did say something about Peach Meadow Canyon."

"Peach Meadow?" Bastian frowned. The canyon was a legend in the red rock country, and Roundy had talked of it. "What did he ask you?"

"If I knew the trail there and if it was passable."

"What did you tell him?"

Sutton threw up his hands. "What could I tell him? I've heard of that canyon ever since I came into this country, and I've looked for it. Who wouldn't, if all they say is true?"

As they moved out Mike put his hand on Dru's arm. "Dru? This is going to be rough, so if you want to go back—?"

"I wouldn't think of it."

"Well, I won't say I'm sorry. I like having you with me. In fact—" His voice trailed off.

There was more he meant to say, and Drusilla realized it. She also knew he was very tired. She had no idea of the brutally hard ride before he arrived at the Ragan ranch or the crossing of the canyon, but she could see the weariness in his face.

They rode side by side when the trail permitted, and Mike explained. "I doubt if Ducrow will stop for anything now. There isn't another good hideout within miles, and he will know he's pursued, although not by whom or how many. I almost wish he knew it was me."

"Why?"

"Because he wants to kill me," he said simply, "and he might stop long enough to try."

CHAPTER 16

THEN THEY WERE alone in the night, with only the horses under them, only the stars to watch. "Is it far?"

"I do not know," he said. "If Ducrow knows where it is he has found the perfect hideaway. Outlaws often stumble across such places in making getaways from the law, or they hear of them from some Indian, some trapper or prospector, and file the knowledge away against future need."

"What is Peach Meadow Canyon?"

"It is said to be near the river, one of those deep canyons that branch off from the Colorado or one of its tributaries. According to the stories somebody discovered it years ago, but the Spanish had been before him, and Indians before them. There are cliff-dweller ruins in the place, but no way to get into it from the plateau. The Indians had a way, and the Spanish are supposed to have reached it by boat.

"The prospector who found it told folks there was fresh water and a small meadow. Somebody had planted some peach trees, probably from pits he carried in his pack. Nobody ever saw him or it again, so the place exists only on his say-so. The Indians now say there's no such place, but they may just not want anybody nosing around. Ducrow might be trying to throw us off, but he might actually know something."

"You'll try to follow him in the dark?"

"No, not actually. It is night and he will be taking it easy as this is rough country. He can't get out of this area where we're traveling, so we'll stay behind him until he leaves the canyon. By that time it will be daylight and we can pick up his trail."

"I am worried for Juliana."

"Of course, but I think he knows somebody is following, so I don't think he will stop until he reaches the canyon or turns into rough country."

For several miles they rode down a high-walled canyon from which there was no escape. Ben Curry and Roundy had both told him of it, as one of the approaches to Walt Sutton's place. Once they emerged from the canyon, however, he must be extremely careful.

At the canyon's end, where it opened upon a wide stretch of semidesert, he pulled up and swung down. "We can't have a fire," he said, "because in this country a man can see for miles, and we want him to think we're pushing hard on his trail."

He put his folded poncho on the ground near a flat-faced boulder and handed Dru a blanket. "Rest," he said. "You'll need it."

She was feeling the chill and gathered it close about her. "Aren't you cold? If we sat close together it would be warmer, and we could share the blanket."

He hesitated, then sat down beside her and pulled the blanket across his shoulders. He was desperately tired but feared to fall asleep. Ducrow might leave Juliana and double back to kill him. He had unsaddled and ground-hitched the horses but had no worry about them drifting off. This was one of the few patches of grass anywhere around.

Yet he did sleep. When the sky was faintly gray he awakened suddenly, listened, looked at the horses who were cropping grass contentedly, and then eased from under the blanket.

He caught the horses, smoothed the hair on their backs with his hand, and saddled up. From time to time he glanced at Dru, who was sleeping peacefully. He was amazed that he should be here, in this lonely place, with this beautiful girl. He, an orphan and foster son of an outlaw.

Some movement of his must have awakened her, for her breath caught and then her eyes opened. She looked up at him with a sleepy smile. "I was tired!" She sat up and watched as he kindled a small fire in the shadow of a boulder. Using very dry wood that would offer almost no smoke, he got his small coffeepot from the pack and started coffee.

Digging into his pack he found some hard biscuits and beef jerky. "Better eat what you can," he said. "We won't be stopping again."

She drew on her boots and stood up, shaking out her hair.

Squatting by the fire he studied the terrain that lay before them, trying to recover from his memory all he had been told about it.

Ducrow would have no trail to find and would have moved swiftly. By now he would probably have reached his goal or was nearing it. When they were in the saddle again they picked up the tracks of the three horses they were following. It was easier because the packhorse Ducrow was leading was a horse Mike remembered, and the tracks were familiar.

What sign there was he could follow from the saddle, and they gained distance, moving swiftly. Dawn broke and the sky was streaked with rose and gold. The warming sun began to ease some of the stiffness from their muscles.

The trail crossed a small valley, skirted an alkali lake and dipped into a maze of boulders and rocky outcroppings before entering a pine forest. Nowhere did he see any signs of a camp. Juliana, who lacked the strength and fire of Drusilla, must be almost dead from fatigue. Obviously, the outlaw knew exactly where he was going and that his destination was not far off. He was making no effort to save his horses.

The trail became more difficult to follow. Mike slowed his pace, then suddenly stopped.

The tracks had vanished as if the three horses had stepped off a cliff!

"Stay in the saddle. I've got to look around a bit."

Mike studied the ground, then walked back to the last tracks he had seen, which he had taken care not to cross in the event he needed to examine them again.

He knew the stride of each horse now, and he measured the distance with his eye, knowing where each hoof must fall.

Nothing . . .

He paused, studying the ground, then the pine timber that surrounded the spot. It seemed absolutely uniform and as he would expect it to be. Avoiding the trail ahead he went into the woods and walked a slow circle around his own horses, studying the ground, the trunks of the trees, everything. He found no tracks.

He stopped, hands on his hips, scowling in concentration. They were gone, and seemed to have left no trail.

Dru was watching him, worried now. She started to speak but he lifted a hand. "Wait! I want to think."

He studied, inch by inch, the trail ahead and the trail on his right. Nothing offered a clue. The three horses and the two riders had vanished as if they had ridden off into space.

On the left the pine woods were thick, so dense as to offer no means of passing through. He had studied the trees and brush, and even if a horseman turned that way there was no place to go.

As the trail ahead was trackless it had to be on the right. Again he walked into the woods, and found no tracks. It was impossible, yet it had happened.

"Could they have backtracked?" Dru asked.

"There were no tracks except those going ahead. I believe—" He stopped, swore softly. "I'm a fool! Lend me your hat."

Puzzled, she removed her hat and handed it to him. Using the hat as a fan he began to wave it over the pine needles, letting the wind he created move the needles. He worked for several minutes, then suddenly stopped.

"Got it!" He pointed. "There they are!"

Dru stepped her horse closer. With the pine needles wafted away, the tracks were plain.

"Ducrow is smart. He rode across the open space, then turned back the way he had come, riding over on the far side close to that wall of pines. Then he dismounted, and probably in his sock feet came back and scattered pine needles over the tracks, letting the wind sift them down naturally."

Mounting again, they started back, but from time to time he dismounted to check for tracks. Suddenly the trail turned into a narrow gap in the pine forest, and they followed, winding their way through thick woods. Once Mike indicated a scar on a tree where a stirrup had brushed.

"Move as quietly as you can," he whispered, "and don't speak aloud. Voices carry. He may try to ambush us."

"Do you think he knows we're following?"

"I'm sure of it, and he knows I'm a tracker but not whether I am any good or not."

The trail was now no longer hard to follow and they made better time. Mike Bastian had a hard time keeping his thoughts from the girl with whom he rode. What would she think when she discovered her father was an outlaw? And that he himself had been raised to be an outlaw?

Pine trees thinned, and before them was a vast misty blue distance. Mike stepped down from the saddle and walked forward on moccasined feet. On the rim of the canyon were a few cedars and a pinyon pine or two. Scouting the rim he stopped suddenly, feeling the hair prickle on the back of his neck.

Had they gone down *that*? He knelt on the rock. Yes, it was the scar of a horse's shoe on the rock. He moved a little further, looking down. The cliff fell away for hundreds of feet, but the trail was there, a rock ledge scarcely three feet wide.

He walked back and explained. Dru nodded. "If you are ready, I am." She paused. "Mike, he may be waiting for us. We may get shot."

He shrugged. "I knew that when I started, Dru. These are rough men, and Ducrow has reason to hate me. Of course, he will try to kill me."

"But you needn't have come, Mike."

He shrugged again. "I didn't think much about it. Your sister was kidnapped. I was there and knew what to do. It is as simple as that."

"Who are you, Mike? Uncle Voyle seemed to know about you, and that man, the one who tried to kill you he knew you. And I heard you say Ben Curry sent you to stop them from raiding the ranch. Who is Ben Curry? And are you an outlaw?"

For as long as a man might have counted to a slow ten Mike looked out over the canyon. "No," he said at last, "I am not an outlaw, although I was raised to be one. Ben Curry raised me like his own son, planning that I should inherit the leadership."

"You lived with them?"

"When I wasn't out in the woods. Ben Curry taught me and had me taught. How to shoot, track, ride, even to open locks and safes."

"What is he like, this Ben Curry?" Dru asked.

Mike hesitated, and then said, "In any other time he might have been considered a great man. In his own way, he is. Back in the days of robber barons he would have wound up with a title, I expect.

"When he came west it was wild, there was little law and much of that was enforced by men big enough to get away with it. If they rustled cattle they were building their herds. If a cowboy did it he was rustling. He had a small outfit and he branded loose cattle like they all did, but the trouble was he wasn't big enough. They came after him and he fought. He fought altogether too well, but that made him an outlaw.

"He accepted the role, but he's one of these men who can do nothing small. Soon he was organizing a bigger outfit, planning the jobs like a general plans a campaign, arranging getaways.

"He no longer went out himself, he was behind the scenes, planning it all. I doubt if any other man could have done it, for outlaws do not take to organization, and when they have money they want to spend it where there are bright lights."

"He has killed men?"

"Two, that I know of. One was a justified killing. The second one? Well, he was in a hurry."

"Are you apologizing for him? After all, he was an outlaw and a killer of men."

"He was all of that, but I am not apologizing for him. He's a man who always stood on his own two feet.

"He may have been wrong but he was always

good to me. He took me in when I had no place to go, and he cared for me."

"Was he a big man, Mike? A big old man?"

His eyes avoided hers. So she knew, then?

"In many ways he was one of the biggest men I ever knew. . . . We'd better get started."

It was like stepping off into space, but the horses accepted it calmly enough. After all, they were mountainbred and would go anywhere as long as there was a foothold.

The canyon gaped to receive them, and they went down the narrow, switchback trail. Here and there Mike could see that work had been done. Somebody with a pick and perhaps high explosives of some kind had made a trail where none had been before.

It was late afternoon when they started down, and soon shadows began to creep up the canyon walls, reaching with hungry fingers for the vanishing sunlight. At a wider spot Mike dismounted and Dru did also. Mike carried his rifle in his right hand, ready for instant use. What was to happen could begin at any moment and he had not wanted to be caught in the saddle on a narrow trail where a wounded horse might rear and fall.

His eyes sought the shadows, searching the canyon below for some sign of a house, for a fire, for movement. He saw nothing.

Supposing they were not here at all? That Ducrow had tricked him somehow?

He shook his head. He could not accept that. He had to be right. He thought of Juliana and Ducrow. She could never cope with such a man. Dru, now—

He grinned despite himself. He had an idea Dru would have made Ducrow wish he'd never been born. She was lovely, but there was steel in her, too.

They could hear the river now, not the roaring that he heard when crossing on the cable, but swift, silent, rushing water. Silent, at least, by comparison.

The tracks led back from the river and into a high-walled, almost hidden canyon. It seemed only a gap in the canyon walls, but it angled off to the east. He followed the tracks. It would soon be dark.

The canyon turned a little and he glimpsed a fire reflecting from canyon walls. He paused and passed the reins to Dru. "You will have to stay with the horses."

"Is—is it them?"

"It couldn't be anyone else." He paused. "I'll have to kill him, you know."

"Don't you be killed."

He started forward and she caught his arm. "Mike, let me go. Maybe he would listen."

"He won't. You know that. I've got it to do."

"Why are you doing this? She isn't your sister."

"No . . . but she's yours."

His moccasins made no sound in the sand or on the rocks. He could see a figure moving about the fire. Then he saw Juliana, her head on her arms, sitting near the fire. Ducrow glanced over at her, then said impatiently, "Get some of this coffee into you! This is where you stay, here in Peach Meadow Canyon. You're my woman now!"

He straightened up from the fire. "Monson an'

Clatt! They ran like scared foxes! No bottom to them! I come for a woman an' I got one!"

"Why don't you let me go?" Juliana lifted a tear-streaked face. "My father is a wealthy man. He will pay you well."

"Your pa? I thought Voyle Ragan was your uncle?"

"He is. My father is Ben Ragan. He ranches north of the canyon."

"North of the canyon? Not unless he's a Mormon, he don't." Suddenly he straightened from the fire again. "What's he look like, this pa of yours?"

"He's a great big man with gray hair, a heavy jaw—" She stopped talking, staring at Ducrow. "What's the matter with you?"

"Your pa, this Ben Ragan—a big man with a scar on his jaw. That him?"

"Oh, yes! Take me to him. He will pay you well!"

Ducrow was laughing. "Well, I'll be damned! So I latched onto the old rooster's chick, did I?" He chuckled sourly. "Now I'm really goin' to enjoy this here. So the old devil had hisself a family, did he? I thought all he had was that damned brat, that Mike Bastian!"

CHAPTER 17

Kim Baca was on the town. It had been three years since he leaned on a bar in Denver, and he had headed for Gahan's opposite the courthouse. He was known there, and friends often dropped in. Moreover, it was a place to pick up news and information, and that was what he wanted.

With money in his pocket and time on his hands, Kim was content. He played a couple of games of pool, bowled a little, had a few drinks here and there, and ate in some of the best restaurants. He spoke to old acquaintances, talked with some of the girls along the street. But it was not until he reached the bar at Gahan's that he actually heard anything.

Kim was young, he was attractive, and he was friendly. He had removed the badge from his vest and carried it in his pocket, as he did not want to inhibit any old friends or arouse suspicion in others.

At Gahan's he ordered a beer and looked around. George Devol was having a drink with two shady-looking characters at a nearby table, and at the other end of the bar Bill Cody was surrounded by a group of friends. It was as Kim had remembered it. He was thinking of another beer when a man stopped beside him and a low voice said, "Rounded up any good stock lately?"

Kim glanced around and found himself looking into Doc Middleton's smiling face. Doc was said to be the most successful horse thief in the West, but they both knew Kim had been every bit as good and perhaps better.

"Not so's you could notice," Kim said. "I resigned in your favor. You were makin' the competition too tough."

Doc chuckled. "Your only trouble was you *loved* fine horses," he said. "I took 'em an' sold 'em and went back for more. You just had to have the best horses in the country, and such horses are remembered. No way you could get away with it."

Doc turned his back to the bar and leaned his elbows on it, watching the crowd. "I see you ain't wearin' your badge. You quit?"

"No," Kim replied. "I think I'm locked in for good, Doc, so do me a favor and stay away from my town, will you? I'd hate to jail an old friend."

"If you could catch me." Doc's expression changed and he turned around, facing the mirror. "You workin' with Bord Chantry?"

"I am."

"I like him. When he was ranchin' down there he always set a good table. I put my feet under it time to time when ridin' the country." Doc turned and looked into his eyes. "This is no time for you to be away from home, Baca. Bord's goin' to need all the help he can get."

"What is it, Doc?"

"You know about Ben Curry's outfit?"

"Just talk around. Not much."

"It's been big, the biggest, but the whisper is that it's breakin' up. The whisper is that the bank in your town is the next one up, and the outfit ridin' that way are sayin' Ben's lost his grip an' that he was a fool, anyway, him wantin' no shootin'."

"When?"

"Next couple of days. Maybe tomorrow. Remember Clatt? Yeah, he's one of them. He's talkin' it around that he's going to kill Bord if Chantry so much as shows on the street."

Doc Middleton touched the spot on Kim's vest where the badge had been pinned. "I never wore one of those, but some of the men who do are mighty square. I've been treated right here an' there.

"Far as that goes"—he spoke more softly—"as I come up the street I ran into Bat Masterson. We shook hands, talked over old buffalo huntin' days, and then he suggested I not stay around Denver too long. Too many people know me.

"He knows I'm wanted, but we also fit a couple of Injun fights together. He's square."

Kim Baca nodded. "Know him myself. He's a good man." His thoughts were racing ahead. He was miles from home and Bord would need him, need him desperately. There was no way—

He swore. Why couldn't he remember the *train*? Just hadn't got used to the idea, and the telegraph, too. He thought the thing through quickly, running over in his mind his every move. First, the telegraph station, then a ticket on the train. "Damn it!" he said bitterly. "I had me a bed in a fine hotel and was fixin' for a late breakfast of whatever was available. Now I got to light out."

"Was I you, with Borden Chantry for a friend, I wouldn't waste around."

Kim finished his beer and left a coin on the bar. "Thanks, Doc. I'll not forget this."

"You just tell Bord that I didn't forget. Monson an' Clatt have never been anything but trouble. Bord Chantry's a good man."

Kim Baca went outside, heading for the railroad. At the despatcher's office he sent his telegram.

NOT FIVE. SEVEN OR EIGHT.
MONSON AND CLATT, TODAY OR TOMORROW.
COMING A-RUNNING.

KB

"When's the next train goin' east?"

The despatcher looked up from under his green eyeshade. "Tomorrow mornin', eight o'clock."

"I need one tonight." Baca flashed his badge. "I need anything that will roll, a place for myself and a horse. Will it help if I call Dave Cook?"

"What's goin' on?"

Briefly, Baca explained. The despatcher replied, "Monson an' Clatt, is it? I'll get the trainmaster. We'll see." He started for the door and over his shoulder he said, "They've robbed trains. Four, maybe five years back Clatt killed one of our boys."

An hour later, with his horse in a stockcar and himself in a caboose, Kim Baca was racing east. With luck he would make it.

There was only the locomotive, the stockcar, and the caboose, but they had a clear track.

There was coffee on the stove. Baca found a cup and helped himself. Somewhere out there Monson and Clatt with several friends were riding for Chantry's town.

He had warned Bord there would be seven or eight but that was guessing. With Ben Curry it was nearly always five men to a job, but Ben was no longer the big man, and Clatt had always run with a gang. He would take all he could get together and they would plan to hit fast and hard.

Monson and Clatt would be shooting to kill.

If Bord got his telegram he would do some planning and round up a couple of good men. The bank was opposite the store, and the building next to the store was the express office. A man placed there could cover the door of the bank and the side door as well. If Bord was at the jail, where his office was, he could cover the bank door as well as the other side of the bank. With a man at the big barn, which was behind the bank and a little further along, they could cover the front, both sides, and the rear.

He finished his coffee and stretched out on a bunk. He was thinking of how the men should be placed and the probable action when he fell asleep.

He was awakened by a slowing of the train. He sat up abruptly. Taking out his watch, he glanced at it. They were scarcely an hour out of Denver.

The brakeman, watching the track, spoke to him. "Baca? Fire up ahead, right alongside the track, one man and a horse. He's tryin' to flag us down."

Baca slung on his gun-belt and picked up his rifle. "One man? Are you sure?"

"Mister, you couldn't hide a sick goat out yonder. It's all wide-open country. This gent looks like he wants a train. There's a dirt ramp there, for loadin' stock, an' he's atop it."

"All right, slow down."

At the brakeman's signal the locomotive slowed down still more. Baca rested his Winchester on the windowsill and waited. He could see the man plainly now, but not his face. But that horse—!

Slowly the train braked to a stop.

"All right, out there! You're covered by a .44 Winchester. So speak your piece!"

"I need a ride for my horse and myself, I am—" The voice broke off. "Baca? Is that you? Sackett, here. There's going to be a holdup."

"That's why I'm headed home. Load up and let's get on with it."

"I was headed your way when I stopped off at the Wiggins place for supper. They've got a telegraph operator at the station there where they load stock. I didn't know of any train, so when the message came through I headed off to join Chantry."

He went to the stove for coffee, hotter and blacker now. Baca filled a cup also and laid out his plan. "I think Bord will have it set up just that way."

"Monson an' Clatt? Tough boys," Sackett said.

Baca sipped his coffee. "With this here telegraph

an' the trains it's gettin' so a poor robber doesn't have much chance."

"It's changing things," Sackett agreed. "Look at us. A couple of years back we wouldn't have a chance of gettin' there in time."

"And we may not now."

The train rumbled along, and the two men alternately slept, drank coffee, and talked, watched the wild countryside slip past them.

Wagon trains had crossed this country, and cattle drives. Before that there were Indians, various branches of the Plains Apache, most of them wiped out by the Comanches.

Baca spoke of it, and Sackett nodded. "More Indians were killed by other Indians than by white men," he said. "I've talked to a few who were the last of their kind."

He peered from the window of the caboose. Antelope went skipping away over the plain, then paused to look back and ran on again. A half dozen buffalo lay on a low hill, watching the train.

"We've got to hope he got that telegram you sent," Tyrel said. "But even so he's a careful man. Nobody's goin' to catch him off guard."

"He knows they've set this place up," Baca agreed.

The brakeman came back over the cars and dropped into the caboose. "Goin' to have to stop for water," he said. "You boys better stand by. Somebody might be wishful of takin' a ride."

The long plains twilight faded as they waited alongside the water tank. The plains stretched out for miles with here and there a gully, and far off a light from a distant window. Somebody else was in the world, anyway.

The brakeman released the water pipe and swung it back into place, tying the rope. Baca and Sackett swung aboard.

"When I first came west," Tyrel Sackett said, "I tied up with a cattle drive, Orrin an' me. Went through to Abilene with it. Then we came on into this country right south of here, rounded up wild cattle, and sold 'em."

"You were in that land-grant fight, weren't you?"*

"Uh-huh. Orrin an' me were. Orrin was sheriff there for a while, too. Then he studied more law and went into politics."

"Best get some sleep. Be daylight before we know it."

"The shack said, I mean the brakeman, that we'd get to town just after daylight."

"Ben Curry always timed his robberies about openin' time at the bank," Baca said. "Fewer folks on the street, and in the bank they're gettin' money out for the day's business."

They dozed, slept, and awakened with gray light in the distance. Tyrel Sackett checked his guns.

Baca walked to the window of the caboose and peered out. For a moment he just looked, and then he said, "Sackett?"

Tyrel turned, struck by an odd sound in his voice. "What is it?"

"Look!"

* As described in *The Daybreakers* by Louis L'Amour.

Tyrel bent to look out.

They were there, three abreast, the others strung out behind. Baca counted aloud. ". . . seven, eight . . . nine. Nine of them. I hope Chantry has some help."

Nine men riding to a town where Borden Chantry waited. "Well," Sackett said quietly, "one thing we know."

"What's that?"

"We're gettin' there on time."

CHAPTER 18

BORDEN CHANTRY FINISHED his coffee and stood up, reaching for his hat. "I'd best get over to the office."

He turned and looked at his wife. "You goin' to be around, Bess?" His eyes met hers. She was as lovely as ever, and never a day passed that he did not thank the good Lord for letting him find her before he made a fool of himself with somebody else.

"Where would I go?"

"Oh, I thought maybe over to Mary's or something."

"I'll be here." She adjusted his coat collar. "Be careful, Borden. You never walk out of that door but that I worry."

"I'll be all right."

A train whistled, and he turned sharply. "That's funny! We don't have any train comin' in this morning."

He glanced out, and he could see it coming, just a locomotive, a stockcar, and a caboose. *Now what the hell?*

He stepped outside and looked toward the station.

The station agent had stepped out on the platform and was shading his eyes along the track. Borden Chantry slipped the thong from the hammer of his gun. He glanced toward the street, but the cafe cut off his view of most of it.

Two men were standing in front of the other cafe, which was across the street, facing toward his house and the railroad. Mary Ann's house was behind it, some distance back, but nobody was stirring there, although a thin trail of smoke rose from the chimney.

The small train was pulling in alongside the unloading ramp, and two men swung down from the caboose before the train was fully stopped.

They ran up the ramp and began opening the stockcar door. One of them was Kim Baca, and the other?

Tyrel Sackett!

Chantry stepped back into the house and took his Winchester from the rack. Bess stared at him, her face gone white.

"Borden? What is it?"

"Trouble," he said, "Kim's back and Sackett with him. They're in a hurry." He checked the rifle, jacked a cartridge into the chamber, and said, "If they stop here, I'm at the office."

"Shouldn't you wait for them?"

"If there's trouble I'd better alert the town. I think it is coming, and fast, or they wouldn't be in such a hurry."

He stepped down off the porch and strode quickly toward the opening between the cafe building and the post office. As he stepped up on the boardwalk he

saw Prissy sweeping the walk in front of the post office.

"Priss," he said quickly, "get off the street. I think
we have trouble coming."

"Borden Chantry, if you think I am afraid—!"

"Priss, there's goin' to be some shootin'. I think
we've got a robbery coming. You get off the street, or
if you want to help, run up the street and tell George
an' Hyatt."

"Not me, marshal! I've my own rifle to get. You
tell them!"

Somebody tugged at his sleeve and Chantry
turned. It was Billy McCoy, a friend of Tom's. "Can
I? Let me!"

"All right. Run up the street and tell them all to
stand by. I think there's going to be an attempted
holdup." He turned and spoke loudly. "Everybody!
Off the street!"

Big Injun, his jailer and occasional deputy, had
come to the jail door, a shotgun in his hands. "Stand
by," Borden said.

He was going to look the fool if nothing happened. After all, Sackett and Baca might be just hur-
rying for breakfast. But why the special train?

He glanced along the street. Three saddle horses
standing in front of the cafe, one down the street in
front of the Mexican cafe. A buckboard at the gro-
cery store. No time to move it now, so the horses
would just have to take their chances.

Kim Baca walked out on the street, hesitated, and
then came over. "They're comin', Bord. We passed

'em just outside of town. There's nine of them, led by Monson an' Clatt."

"How far?"

"How far away? They should be ridin' into town any minute unless our train scared 'em, but I doubt it."

Two miles out of town Monson drew up to let the others gather around him. "You boys know the drill. Clatt, me, an' Porky will ride up the street to the bank. Klondike, you come in from behind the Corral Saloon and hold our horses. The rest of you boys cover the street."

"What if there's trouble?"

"You got a gun. The old man ain't in charge now," Monson said. "Me an' Clatt are. We'll show this bunch what we're made of."

"All right," Clatt said impatiently. "Let's go!"

Klondike hesitated. "Monny, what about that train? I didn't like the looks of it."

"Forget it! Just shiftin' a stockcar in to pick up some cattle. Let's go!"

BORDEN CHANTRY WAS in his office door with the jail behind him. Big Injun was at the window. Hyatt Johnson, up at the bank, had been a major in the Confederate cavalry, and George Blazer at the express office had been a sharpshooter with Sherman and was a veteran of a number of Indian battles.

He glanced down the street. Here they were, three men riding abreast, coming right up the street. A trail of dust where one man had cut over behind the saloon.

"Big Injun?" He spoke over his shoulder. "There's one comin' up behind the Corral. You take him."

Borden Chantry stepped out of the door and went to the edge of the boardwalk.

Down the street Tyrel Sackett, his badge in plain sight, stepped out from the shadow of the McCoy house as the last two riders rode into town. The others were a good fifty yards ahead of them and intent on the street and the town.

"Boys? I'm Tyrel Sackett, and I'd like to talk to you. Get down off those horses and come over here. And boys? Keep your hands in sight."

Tyrel Sackett? *The Mora gunfighter?*

Denny Dinsmore felt himself go a little sick in the stomach. What the hell was this? Sackett here?

He hesitated. Sweat broke out on his brow. Clyde Bussy was beside him, and Clyde was a good, tough boy, but—

"What is this?" he protested.

Sackett's tone was sharp. "Get off those horses and get over here. *Now!*"

"You want us to drop our gun-belts?" Denny asked.

Sackett seemed to smile, but it was not a smile Denny liked. Why did he ever want to be an outlaw, anyway?

"Oh, no! Keep your guns on! I'd never like it said that I shot an unarmed man!"

Clyde wasn't offering any argument. Slowly and carefully, the two men dismounted.

When the three advance riders drew almost abreast of Chantry, he lifted his left hand. "Just a minute, boys! I'm Borden Chantry, the sheriff. I'd like a word with you."

Something clicked in Monson's brain. *Chantry?* It was his place where the horses were. What had happened? An old man named Riggin was supposed to be marshal here.

Monson laughed. "Sorry, mister sheriff, we ain't got time to talk. Supposin' you just shuck them guns an' walk ahead of us. Walk slow, up to the bank. That all right with you?"

Monson turned in his saddle. "Anybody shows along the street, shoot 'em!"

Monson was cocky, and he was sure of himself. No hick-town sheriff—

He never saw the draw. Borden Chantry had stood there, big, formidable, his gun in his holster. Monson went for his gun but as Chantry drew he stepped to the left, and Monson shifted his gun to cover him, firing as he did so, and he shot his horse, the bullet grazing the black's neck. The horse plunged and Monson was already falling.

There was a burst of gunfire all along the street, the stab of flame from pistols, plunging, rearing horses, the smell of gunsmoke.

Riding from behind the Corral Saloon to become the horse holder while the robbery took place, Klondike heard the shots, saw Monson down, his horse racing away up the street. Somebody was shooting from the bank, and he saw a man kneeling in front of the express office with a Big Fifty Sharps. This was no place for a man who wanted to spend his old age sitting in the sun. Klondike wheeled his horse and headed for the shelter of a barn, from which point he hoped to make the wide-open country beyond.

Klondike had never heard of Big Injun, a big, slow-moving, quiet man who rarely smiled. He did not know that the year Klondike was born Big Injun had taken his ninth scalp. All Klondike knew was that things had exploded all around him and he wanted to get away from there, and fast. He turned his horse to go and the horse made at least two jumps in the right direction. Big Injun, kneeling in the doorway, fired his Sharps, and the bullet, because of the movements of the horse, was a little low. It grazed the cantle of Klondike's saddle and, badly deformed, careened upward. The jagged metal took off the back of Klondike's skull.

What remained of Klondike stayed in the saddle for a quarter of a mile before it fell, toppling into the dust. The horse ran off a little way and, missing its rider, stopped, trotted off a few steps, and waited.

Klondike lay where he had fallen. Klondike, a tough man, was tough no longer. He stared up at the sky. "I wish . . . I just wish . . ."

The sun faded and a grasshopper leaped to his shirtfront, then hopped again. A few yards off his horse started to graze.

Back in the street Clatt, who had always been proud of his silver belt buckle, had no chance to regret it. Up the street George Blazer was kneeling beside a post on the boardwalk in front of the express office. His days with Sherman were long since gone, but his skill with a rifle was not.

The belt buckle flashed an invitation and George accepted it. He was a quiet man who liked to read his newspaper over coffee in the evening, but he did not like a bunch of would-be tough men shooting up his hometown. You could have laid a silver dollar over the spot where the two rifle bullets went in, but you couldn't have covered with a bandana the place where they emerged.

Clatt was down, and nobody knew who accounted for the other two, as several men were shooting and all showed evidence of skilled marksmanship.

Suddenly the thunder of guns, suddenly the flashes of gunfire, the plunging horses, the shouts, cries, dust, and then silence with the smell of dust and gunsmoke.

A horse walked away up the street. Another ran away between the buildings. Others, faithful to their training, stood where their reins had fallen.

Borden Chantry thumbed cartridges into his almost empty gun. People emerged on the street. Prissy came from the post office. "Sheriff Chantry! You should be ashamed of yourself! What did we elect you for! So this sort of thing wouldn't happen! What will people say?"

"I'm sorry, ma'am," Borden said. "We tried to spread the word that this was a quiet town. I'm afraid somebody didn't get the message."

Big Injun, his rifle across the desk, came outside. "I'll get the buckboard an' pick 'em up."

Tyrel Sackett came up the street with two frightened outlaws. They stared at the fallen bodies, faces gray. Denny Dinsmore felt like throwing up. He didn't want to, not in front of all these people.

Clatt and Monson, dead.

Kim Baca was looking at his gun. He had fired two shots and could not remember when or how. He had no idea whether he had even hit anything.

Denny licked his dry lips. "What's for us?" he asked, glancing at Chantry.

Men who tried to steal the money others worked hard to earn got no sympathy from him. "For you? If you're lucky you may get no more than twenty years."

Denny stared at him. Denny was twenty-two. He had thought an outlaw's career would be wild and exciting. He turned and stared at the bodies in the street. He had never really liked any of those men, especially Monson. He had always been a little afraid of Monson, but he had eaten with them, told stories and talked, he had slept in bunkhouses with them and in camps.

Now they were dead.

Twenty *years*? Why, he would be over forty when he got out! His youth gone. He'd be an old man, he'd—

What about Mag? Why, she would never even know what happened to him! And after a little while she wouldn't care.

"Mister," he pleaded. "I—"

"You put your money on the wrong card," Chantry

said. "You dealt your own hand, and in this life a man pays to learn. You just didn't learn fast enough."

He walked away and held out his hand to Sackett. "Thanks," he said. "Thanks very much."

"I'll buy you a drink," Tyrel said, "or coffee."

"Later," Borden said. "I'd better go speak to the wife first. She'll have heard all that shootin'."

She was standing waiting, her face white and still. "Borden? Bord? Are you all right?"

"All right, Bess. They were going to rob the bank. We had to stop them before somebody got hurt. We stopped them."

"You're all right? You're sure?"

"I'm all right, Bess. I will have to go back and see everything straightened up, though. There was some shooting."

"I heard. Was anybody—? I mean, was—?"

"Some outlaws. Tyrel Sackett arrested two of them. There were some pretty bad men among them. Some men just can't understand there isn't any free ride. Everything has its price."

"I can't stand it, Borden. I just can't! I'm not cut out for this. Borden, I want to go home. I want to go back East! I want to get away from all this!"

"I know, Bess, but what would I do back there?"

"I don't care. Anything is better than this!"

"Well"—he turned away—"I'll give it some thought, honey. Now I've got to go finish my job."

He walked to the cafe and stopped outside. Already the bodies were gone, dust thrown over the blood, the loose horses tied up.

What could he do back East? What would he do?

Sackett stood in the door of the Bon-Ton. "Come on in, Bord. Hyatt Johnson's here, and George. We'll have some coffee."

He turned toward the door, looking back once more. This was his town, and it was safe once more.

CHAPTER 19

FIRELIGHT FLICKERED ON the canyon walls, somewhere in the distance a coyote howled. Wind stirred through the pines and fluttered the flame of the fire.

"You set up an' eat. You an' me, we're goin' to have a long time together. How long you live depends on how I get treated, understand? You give me any back talk or any trouble an' I'll kill you.

"Wouldn't be the first woman I killed, although the others were squaws. I never had nothin' like you."

"You will hang for this."

He chuckled harshly. "Yeah? Who is goin' to know it ever happened? You sure ain't goin' to be in no shape to tell anybody, an' who could find this place? Nobody's been in here for fifty year! Maybe more'n that."

Out in the darkness a horse stamped and blew. Ducrow straightened up from the fire, listening.

"Monson an' them," he said, thinking aloud, "I'll bet they went to do that bank job! Well, that will be an easy one! Then if they are smart they'll head for Mexico."

He glanced around at Juliana. "Your pa thought he was king bee!" He paused, then shook his head. "And for a while there, he was. He could plan 'em, I'll give him that." He glanced at Juliana. "Your pa's dead, you know. Perrin an' them, they'll have killed him by now. I mean whoever Perrin left to do it. There was nobody but him, all alone in that stone house of his."

Juliana sat up straighter. "Don't be too sure," she said, "and when he has time he'll hunt you down. Don't you suppose he knows this place? Who knows this country better than he does?"

Ducrow stared at her. "What makes you think he knows this place?"

"Peach Meadow Canyon?" Juliana was frightened, but desperation was making her think. "I've heard him speak of it," she lied.

Ducrow was uneasy now, and she sensed the doubt. He had believed himself secure, but her comment had injected an element of uncertainty. If she had a chance it lay in that doubt. He had believed himself secure, but if she could make him wary, make him hesitate—

"Aw, he don't know nothin' about this place! Nobody does! Anyway, those boys back at Toadstool have taken care of him. All that damn' discipline! Do this, don't do that! Makes a man sick! This here's been comin' for months!"

"The man you call Perrin," Juliana said, "was killed! I looked back. He was down, and Mike Bastian was standing over him."

Ducrow squatted by the fire. Rig Molina would be killed attempting to rob the treasure train, Monson and Clatt were gone, and if Perrin was dead, then what would stop him from moving in and taking over?

Juliana had been afraid but was so no longer. She was like a trapped animal fighting for its life. Dru would have known what to do . . . but what *would* she do? There had to be something, some way to outwit him, some way to trick him . . . How?

The fire—if she could only get him into the fire! If she could trip him, push him! If she could get hold of a gun! She could shoot, even if not so well as Dru.

Or a knife, something she could hide until the proper moment. Even a sharp blade of stone. Indians used them, and some of the scrapers she had seen seemed hardly to have been shaped at all. Her eyes searched the ground for a sharp-edged stone.

She would slash him across the face . . . no, not the face. It must be the throat. She must try to kill him or hurt him badly, she must—

"Here! Eat up, damn you! I haven't time to be stallin' around! Eat!

"Come daylight we're movin' further up the canyon! There's a place—"

"This is the place, Ducrow. Right here!"

He couldn't believe it. Ducrow put the frying pan down and slowly he straightened. Was the thong off his gun or not?

"Ol' Roundy was right." Ducrow was stalling for the moment he wanted. "He said you could track a snake across a flat rock.

"Well, now that you're here, what are you goin' to do about it?"

"Whatever you like, Ducrow, but I'd suggest you just carefully unfasten your belt and let your guns drop. If you don't want to do that you can always shoot it out."

"You're too soft, Bastian! You'll never make a gang leader like ol' Ben was! Ben would never have said aye, yes, or no, he'd just have come in blasting! You got a sight to learn, youngster. You're too soft! Too bad you ain't goin' to live long enough to learn it.

"Perrin always thought he was good with a gun. Never a day in his life I couldn't have beat him!" He lifted his right hand and wiped it across his tobacco-stained beard. The right made a careless gesture but at the same time his left hand dropped to his gun. It came up, spouting flame!

Mike Bastian simply palmed his gun and fired. It was smooth, it was fast, but most important it was accurate. He fired and then stepped to Ducrow's left and fired again.

Ducrow stood staring at him and then his gun dropped from loose fingers. His knees sagged and he fell forward, facedown in the sand. One hand fell into the fire and his sleeve began to smolder. Bastian stepped forward and pushed the hand away from the fire with his toe.

Then he loaded his gun and holstered it.

Dru came running, rifle in hand. "Oh, Mike! I thought you'd been killed! I thought—!

"*Juliana!*" She dropped on her knees beside her

sister, and Mike walked back to the horses. For a long moment he stood leaning on the saddle.

After a while he heard the girls coming and he said, "There's the ruins of a stone house over yonder. Go there. I'll come along in a minute and build a fire. We'll go home in the morning."

He went to where Ducrow lay, and dragged him over against a low ridge of sand and gravel. Then he caved sand over him. "That's good enough for now, Ducrow. When we come back, I'll bury you right and proper."

The coffee was already made, so he brought it to the new fire he built.

Later, as the coals burned down, Dru asked, "Mike? What will you do now?"

"Go back to Toadstool," he said. He sipped his coffee and stared into the cup, then at her. "I've got to go back to Ben. I've got to make sure he's all right."

"And then?"

"Go someplace and start over."

"Not as an outlaw?"

"I never was one, never really wanted to be one." He looked up at her. "Dru, folks have to live together, and it can only be done if they work together to keep things right. There's no room for outlaws in a decent world, not even the kind of world they would try to create.

"Ben was wrong. Wrong from the start, and even as a small boy, I knew it."

"So?"

"He was all I had. I'd no place else to go, and he was kind. I'll say that for him. He was always kind."

SUNLIGHT LAY WHITE upon the empty street at Toad-stool Canyon when Mike Bastian rode into the lower end of town, his rifle across his saddle. Beside him was Dru Ragan.

Juliana had stayed behind at the Ragan ranch, but Dru refused. Ben Curry was her father and she was going to him, regardless, outlaw camp or not. Besides, she would be returning with Mike beside her.

If Dave Lenaker had arrived, Mike thought, the town was quiet enough for it. No horses stood at the hitching rails, and the door of the saloon gaped wide.

Something fluttered in the light wind, and Mike's eyes flickered. Torn cloth on a dead man's shirt, a man he did not know.

He walked his horse up the silent street, and the hoof falls were loud in the stillness. A man's hand and wrist lay across a windowsill. A pistol lay on the ground beneath it. There was blood on the stoop of another house.

"There's been a fight," Mike said softly, "and a bad one. Better get yourself set for the worst."

At the mess hall a man lay sprawled in the doorway.

They drew up at the foot of the stone steps and Mike helped her down. "Stay a little behind me, if you must come."

Up the steps, across the wide veranda, and into the

huge living room. Shocked, they stopped in their tracks.

Five men sat about a table, playing cards. A coffee-pot bubbled on the stove.

Doc Sawyer, Roundy, Garlin, and Colley were there, Garlin's head was bandaged, and Colley had one leg stretched out stiff and straight, as did Ben Curry, who was on the sofa. All were smiling.

Dru ran to her father and dropped on her knees beside him. "Oh, Dad! We were so scared!"

"What happened?" Mike demanded. "Did Dave Lenaker get here?"

"He surely did, but what do you think? It was Rigger Molina who got him! The Rigger got to Weaver and discovered Perrin had double-crossed him before he ever made an attempt on the train. When he found out that Perrin had lied about the number of guards on the treasure train he simply rode back.

"When he found that Ben was crippled and Perrin had run out, with Lenaker coming, he waited for Lenaker himself!

"He was wonderful, Mike! I never saw anything like it! He paced the veranda like a bear in a cage, muttering and waiting for Lenaker. 'Leave you in the lurch, will they? I'll show 'em! Lenaker thinks you're gettin' old, does he?'

"They shot it out in the street down there, and Lenaker beat him to the draw. He put two bullets into Rigger, but he wouldn't go down. He just stood there spraddle-legged in the street and shot until both guns were empty.

"Lenaker must have hit him at least five times but when Lenaker himself went down Molina went over and spat in his face. 'That's for a double-crosser!' he said. Mike, he was magnificent!"

"They fooled me, Mike," Roundy said. "I saw trouble comin' and figured I'd better get to old Ben. I never figured on them slippin' in behind and grabbin' you.

"Then I heard Lenaker was comin'. I knew him and I was afraid of what he would do, so I headed down the trail to meet him. Mike, I never killed a man in my life except some Blackfeet that attacked us when I was livin' with the Crows, but I was sure aimin' to kill Lenaker.

"Then Lenaker come in by the old creek trail, and him and his boys went after Ben and the gold he was supposed to have."

"Doc was here," Garlin said, "an' Colley. Roundy slipped through and joined us. Oh, it was some fight while it lasted. We got scratched up some, but nothin' to what they got."

Briefly, Mike Bastian described his fight with Kerb Perrin and the pursuit of Ducrow.

"They've pulled out," Roundy said, "all that's alive."

"The only man who ever fooled me was Rigger Molina," Ben Curry said. "I never guessed he was that loyal, but he took that fight when I was in no shape to, and soaked up lead like a sponge soaks water."

Doc Sawyer idly shuffled the cards. "Ben," he

said, "I think we should move out, as soon as you're able to ride. I think we should all move out."

Ben Curry looked up at Dru. "Now you know. Your old man's an outlaw. I never wanted you to know, and I planned to get shut of this whole outfit and live out my days with your ma, over there on the V-Bar."

"Why don't you?" Dru asked.

"Funny," Ben said, "I never figured it would get this big, never at all. One thing just follered another until it got too big to let go of."

"It was over, Ben. You held men together who did not like being held. You made things work. Now some of them will slip away and probably disappear just like you can."

"You shuffle them cards any more, Doc," Garlin said, "and I'll get worried what you're doin' to that deck. Set up an' deal."

Mike and Dru walked outside and looked down over Toadstool Canyon. There were no lights in the town where dead men lay, sprawled in their last moments.

Inside they heard argument. "He's a fine lad, Ben, and well educated, if I do say so who taught him all he knows."

"All he knows!" Roundy exploded. "Book larnin' is all well an' good but where would that gal be tonight if'n I hadn't taught him to read sign an' foller a trail? I ask you, where would she be?"

On the wide veranda, with the stars brushed by the dark fingertips of the pines, Mike said to Dru, "I can read sign, all right, but I'm no hand at reading the trail to a woman's heart. You will have to help me, Dru."

She laughed, resting a hand on his arm. "Mike, you've been blazing that trail ever since we met in Weaver! You need no help at all!"

She turned him to face her. "Mike, I love this country! Every bit of its red rock canyons, its green cedars, the pines, the distance . . . all of it! Why don't we get some cattle and go back to Peach Meadow Canyon?

"Why don't we build a cabin, plant some more peaches, and start a place of our own? You said you could make a better trail better than the one we used."

From inside Garlin was saying, "Monson an' Clatt? Wherever they went, we'll hear of them soon enough!"

"That Clatt," Ben commented, "he was one I was going to drop. Liked to brag too much! He wanted to tell around the saloons what a tough man he was. He wasn't content with my kind of operation, wanted to be pointed out as a bad man and an outlaw."

"The trouble with that," Garlin remarked, "is that the law listens, too." He glanced at Ben Curry. "He favored that bank back over the mountains. He always did think well of that job."

Curry glanced at his cards. He would keep what he had. He looked over them at Garlin. "I was calling it off. The old marshal, Riggin was his name, he got himself killed, and that rancher where we left the horses, Borden Chantry was his name, he took over as marshal."

He watched Doc draw two cards. Three of a kind, maybe?

"There at their wagon I drank coffee with Chantry. I looked across my cup at him and I knew then he was one man I wanted no part of. When he became marshal I decided I'd just forget that job. Not that I didn't think back to it every now and again, but it always came up as a bad bet."

"Come daylight," Doc said casually as he laid down three nines and took the pot, "we should ride out of here. If somebody happened by there'd be explanations." He stacked his winnings in neat piles. "I'm glad it's over, Ben. You an' me, we're the past. Those youngsters outside there, they are tomorrow."

Ben hitched himself into a more comfortable position. "You're right, of course. All of us, you, me, Wyatt Earp, Billy the Kid, Bill Hickok, we've lived out our time in a world we never made.

"Take Billy now, I knew him as a youngster. Not a bad kid, but in Lincoln County them days you took sides. You had to. Billy took the right side, too. Tunstall and Maqueen were good men, and then of the whole two hundred or so involved in that fight Billy was the only one ever brought to trial."

Garlin, gathering the cards, suddenly stopped. On the back of a nine of spades there was a small fingernail scratch. Quickly he ran through the deck. There was another on the nine of diamonds, a third on the nine of hearts.

"Doc!" he yelled. "Damn you for a four-eyed pirate! You—!"

Ben chuckled and hitched himself around to get

his foot on the floor. "Gar, you ought to know Doc by now. With him it ain't the money, it's the winning. How many times has he staked you?"

Garlin shrugged, smiling. "Nevertheless—"

Out in the dark a coyote pleaded plaintively to the silent stars, and Ben heaved himself to his feet, leaning on the heavy cane.

On the porch, nearing the low stone wall, Mike Bastian stood with Dru. He stood staring for a minute, then muttered, "Well, why not?"

He looked down the dark and empty street. Tomorrow it would be alone with its ghosts.

"Garlin?" Mike called out. "See that Rig Molina gets a proper marker, will you? Say *He was a good man.* And carve it in stone."

WHAT IS LOUIS L'AMOUR'S
LOST TREASURES?

Louis L'Amour's Lost Treasures is a project created to release some of the author's more unconventional manuscripts from the family archives.

Currently included in the series are *Louis L'Amour's Lost Treasures: Volume 1,* published in the fall of 2017, and *Volume 2,* which was published in the fall of 2019. These books contain both finished and unfinished short stories, unfinished novels, literary and motion picture treatments, notes, and outlines. They are a wide selection of the many works Louis was never able to publish during his lifetime.

In 2018 we released *No Traveller Returns,* L'Amour's never-before-seen first novel, which was written between 1938 and 1942. In the future, there may be a selection of even more L'Amour titles.

Additionally, many notes and alternate drafts to Louis's well-known and previously published novels and short stories will now be included as "bonus feature" postscripts within the books that they relate to. For example, the Lost Treasures postscript to *Last of the Breed* will contain early notes on the story, the short story that was discovered to be a missing piece of the novel, the history of the novel's inspiration and creation, and information about unproduced motion picture and comic book versions.

An even more complete description of the Lost Treasures project, along with a number of examples of what is in the books, can be found at louislamourslosttreasures.com. The website also contains a good deal of exclusive material, such as pieces of unknown stories that were too short or too incomplete to include in the Lost Treasures books, plus personal photos, scans of original documents, and notes.

All of the works that contain Lost Treasures project materials will display the Louis L'Amour's Lost Treasures banner and logo.

LOUIS L'AMOUR'S LOST TREASURES

POSTSCRIPT

by Beau L'Amour

HAVING A CHANCE to discuss the history of *Son of a Wanted Man* gives me an excellent opportunity to delve into the subject of how my father and I each adapted the story to different mediums, and it will also tell the story of Dad's involvement in the creation of the Bantam Books Audio Publishing program. First, however, it's important for me to explain exactly where this novel came from. . . .

The plot, and many of the characters, originated with a novella, "The Trail to Peach Meadow Canyon." Novellas—or, as they were sometimes called, "magazine novels"—were a good deal longer than the typical 10-to-20-page short story, yet somewhat shorter than the 140-to-220-page paperback novels on which Dad was to build his career from the 1950s through the 1980s. Since magazines paid by the word, writing a novella allowed the writer to make more money off of a single story idea, but it had the downside of being harder to sell. Overall, the pulp magazines had considerably fewer available slots for these magazine novels, so there was a certain amount of risk involved when a writer chose to experiment with longer material.

This novella was written in either the latter part of 1948 or early '49. It was an interesting period in Dad's life because he was just beginning to recognize the limits of his current career. He was writing full out, creating as much material as he possibly could, often a story a week, and a good deal of it was getting published. Financially, however, he was nowhere near where he wanted to be. Something had to change.

And something *was* changing . . . but not in a good way. Due to pressure from TV, radio, and particularly from the growing medium of paperback books, the pulp magazine business was beginning to collapse.

Experimenting with longer work was not only Dad's way of reducing the demands of having to come up with so many new story ideas; it was, hopefully, the beginning of a shift into a career of writing novels. Step one was to try creating novellas for the pulps and, in doing so, perhaps buy himself a cushion of time and money to write even longer material. Step two would be the move to become a full-time novelist. This was a goal Dad had wanted to achieve since he wrote the earliest drafts of No Traveller Returns in the late 1930s. It is true that in the latter part of 1949, he was able to write the novel Westward the Tide. But that attempt to balance time against money backfired. The book wasn't published in the United States until the 1970s, and the loss of time, and therefore income, forced Dad to take on the Hopalong

Cassidy novel series in order to keep from going hungry. He would not be able to make the move into the paperback market until the money from the movie option to his short story "The Gift of Cochise," which became *Hondo,* bought him some breathing room in the early 1950s.

"The Trail to Peach Meadow Canyon" was released in *Giant Western* magazine in the fall of '49. The editor was kind enough to compare it in print to Zane Grey's *Lone Star Ranger,* though that was probably more of a marketing gimmick than anything else. At some point, the story was briefly titled "The Arizona Strip," a reference to the triangle of territory from the north bank of the Colorado River to the state borders of Utah and Nevada. This area was at one time isolated from Arizona's law enforcement officers by the lack of ways to cross the river, and it was outside the jurisdiction of the other two states. Both Ben Curry's hideout and Peach Meadow Canyon were supposedly located in this wild, lawless tract of land.

Here's how Dad described visiting some of the areas that inspired the fictional locations he created for his story:

```
Shortly after WWII when living in Los
Angeles I often took the train or bus to
one of the towns near Grand Canyon.
Several times it was Peach Springs,
Arizona. I knew no one there but would
get off the bus and back pack into the
canyons branching off from the Grand
```

Canyon and spend three or four days
hiking wild country, alone. Most of my
friends or acquaintances had jobs from
which they could not get away and not
many of them would accept the rugged
conditions I took for granted. Another
place I often went was the wilderness
area of Sycamore Canyon. In those days
there was a small railroad, the Verde-
Mix, I believe it was called, and for a
couple of dollars one could buy a ticket
and the train crew would drop you off and
pick you up later. Several times I went
up into the Sycamore Canyon area,
exploring, camping, simply living the
life. It is a beautiful area, near Oak
Creek Canyon and Sedona.

In the introduction to "The Trail to Peach Meadow
Canyon" when it was republished in the 1986 collection *The Rider of the Ruby Hills*, he took the description a bit further:

Peach trees have been found growing in
several of the canyons branching off from
the Grand Canyon; they were probably
planted by someone sometime in the past.
I ventured into a box canyon in Arizona
at one time, a place enclosed by high
cliffs with some sixty acres of fairly
level ground in the bottom, a good stand
of grass, and about three dozen peach and

apricot trees, all old and in need of
pruning. There was also a half dugout
built of logs against the side of a low
mound, and a stream about two feet wide
running diagonally across the bottom of
the canyon.

And interestingly, he then added:

Not far from Mooney Falls in the Grand
Canyon, there are iron ladders spiked to
the walls to enable one to climb further
down.

It's odd that he just tacked this on there; it's almost
a non sequitur. But I have some vague memories about
this reference. The ladders either allowed access to
the river from a nearby cabin, or led upward to the
rim of the canyon. My father may have met the man
who was living there. I remember Dad telling me
something about how the man said he carried a pistol
for all the normal reasons but also because he feared
someday he would have a fall and break a leg . . . and
he didn't want to starve to death. It's a random memory from Louis's life that would have been lost—and
I certainly wouldn't have remembered—if he hadn't
included a reference to it in that introduction.

While none of the locations just mentioned were
on the northern or "Arizona Strip" side of the Grand
Canyon, he did, eventually, discover a place that fit
this description even better. In 1983, just before we
left on a research trip for *The Haunted Mesa,* he

made an entry in his journal about starting the process of adapting "The Trail to Peach Meadow Canyon" into the novel *Son of a Wanted Man*. He wrote:

> It [the story] speaks of a canyon almost
> a duplicate for Johnnie's Hole [a
> location used in *The Haunted Mesa*] except
> for the peach trees, but I shall take
> care of that aspect.

I have no memory of Dad spreading peach pits while we were in Johnnies Hole, but he did save them up and plant them in various other places. The notable thing here is that, although it's in Utah, Johnnies Hole *is* north of the Colorado River, closer to the location he had in mind than the canyons with the peach trees on the south side.

In order to adapt "The Trail to Peach Meadow Canyon," to make it long enough to fit into the paperback novel format, Dad added in the Sackett and Chantry subplot. This gave him a chance to use characters his fans would enjoy, and it also illustrated the theme that Ben Curry's time as an outlaw was over. Mike Bastian was making a wise choice to not follow in his adoptive father's footsteps. These changes, as well as some new character names and various other polishes, were quickly made, and the novel version was released as *Son of a Wanted Man* in 1984. It went on to sell quite well . . . and it still does.

AT THIS POINT our story shifts onto a number of side-tracks, the first of them into the realm of movie adaptations. In that same year, 1984, I graduated from California Institute of the Arts with a degree in film. Live action film, to be precise. CalArts was funded by the Disney family, and thus it is perhaps better known for its character animation program, as well as for film graphics (meaning visual effects, the predecessor of today's CGI). It was definitely an odd place, and ground zero for some of the strange trends that have since shown up in the Disney organization; however, there is no question I got an excellent education.

One of my two faculty mentors was Alexander Mackendrick, a Scottish writer, producer, and director who was easily the greatest teacher I've ever had. Arrogant and irascible, he terrified quite a few of our current well-known directors—and carefully molded them. On the kindlier end of the spectrum was Ed Emshwiller, a man I easily connected with because he had spent a good deal of his career illustrating science fiction paperbacks and magazines. Ed had worked painting book covers for several of the art directors I had known at Bantam Books. Later, while working at the New York Institute of Technology, he had created, along with Pixar founder Alvy Ray Smith, the very first piece of computer-generated animation, *Sunstone,* in 1979. Last, and you'll see why this matters in a few pages, there was one of my favorite teachers, Don Worthen. Don ran the institute's postproduction sound department and taught me many techniques I put to good use later on.

So, full of (possibly misplaced) ambition, I threw

myself into Hollywood's job market, doing everything that came my way: driving trucks, breaking
down soundtracks to prepare them for mix sessions,
and being a production assistant. Among other
things, I spent a year working for a production company called Finnegan Associates as a sort of junior
producer. It was Bill Finnegan who gave me the best
definition I've ever heard of what a movie producer
actually does: "whatever it takes."

My time working for Bill, his wife, Patricia, partner Sheldon Pinchuk, and their whole crew was wonderful. They were very tolerant of my mistakes, and
when I showed initiative, like hiring a number of my
friends, I got the freedom to run with it. However,
the pace was exhausting. In the year I was there, they
produced more than a dozen films, with a very limited staff. Everyone pitched in on everything, and we
were all involved in projects we were never credited
on. There were months and months of seventeen-
hour days, and by the time their schedule slowed and
a number of us were let go, I was grateful. I probably
slept for a week.

A couple of months later I ended up working for a
friend, John Putch, as location sound mixer (which
means I was recording on-set dialogue) on a short
film he was directing titled "Waiting to Act." For a
short, it was kind of amazing, as the cast was packed
with film and TV veterans like Helen Hunt, Ed Beg-
ley, Jr., Jonathan Prince, Mary McDonough, and Jean
Stapleton. The lead role was played by a guy named
Charles Van Eman. Over the course of the production, he and I struck up a friendship, mostly talking

about writing. At some point we began discussing writing something together.

That "something" was to become the screenplay for *Son of a Wanted Man* . . . or "The Trail to Peach Meadow Canyon" . . . or . . . well, this is where we have to take another sidetrack and dig down into the realities of scriptwriting.

ALTHOUGH TODAY WE see many feature films that run close to three hours, and "hour-long" streaming or cable episodes sometimes clock in at over sixty minutes, in those days the running time of everything was strictly enforced. The rough rule of thumb is that the average screenplay runs a page a minute. In the theaters they used to like to start a new showing every two to two and a half hours . . . and that included trailers, credits, and getting the audience into and out of their seats. So if a writer turned in a script that was much over 120 pages, it was considered unprofessionally long. A movie that was too long meant the theater would lose a showing, or even two, every day . . . and that was money down the drain. The preference was for something in the range of 90 to 110 pages, with a hope that the final cut would come in around one hundred minutes at most.

In TV the rules were even more strict. Starting out in 1982, the first film I worked on was an old-school network Movie of the Week, or MOW. If I remember correctly, that script was required to be exactly 94 pages, to fill a two-hour time slot. The remaining twenty-six minutes were there for commercials, network identification, credits, and things like that. In 2001, right at the end of the made-for-TV-movie era, I was involved with another project, and the distributor required an 89-page script. Given that a typical dialogue scene averages about two minutes, with some of them running five minutes or more, the screenwriter is going to have to tell the entire story in forty to sixty scenes. That's all a bit technical, but the bottom line is that in film you have to tell the story as efficiently as possible.

And that brings us back to the screenplay that Charlie and I were going to write. One of the first rules you learn in adaptation is to get rid of every story element you can find a way to live without. You have to strip it down to its essentials. For *Son of a Wanted Man,* that meant the Sackett and Chantry scenes had to go. There were other, simpler ways to illustrate that the West was changing and Ben Curry's outlaw days were numbered. And a technical issue made that decision even easier: Character rights are generally transferred along with movie rights. Tyrel Sackett had already appeared in NBC's *The Sacketts,* and while we were still lucky enough to have a contractual claim to those characters, jumping through all the hoops to prove those rights would have been uselessly expensive. In the case of Borden Chantry, it seemed foolish to create a similar legal snarl, just so he could play a minor part in this script. So the first step in the adaptation was to look for inspiration in the more reasonably sized—and less complex—novella "The Trail to Peach Meadow Canyon." At the same time, we wanted to use the name *Son of a Wanted Man* because it is a far better title.

Charlie and I put together a rough outline, and then a very detailed treatment. A treatment is more of a description of a story, rather than the story itself, and the tone is often fairly clinical. It's a good way to plan out a script in great detail, and it is a good reality check to figure out what is actually going to be in the story rather than what you simply imagined ought to be there. In addition, when collaborating with another writer, it's always an advantage to get all the details down right in the beginning; that way, you both understand what is going on in every scene.

The best literature is created by a writer stimulating the reader's imagination to do a significant amount of the creative work. But when you are adapting to a medium that is fairly literal, like movies, elements will always be lost or executed in a manner that doesn't meet an audience's expectations. No movie can ever be like the book, because the reader's mind does its best to make the reading experience the perfect version of the story. In movies compromises always have to be made. The best you can hope for is that if you make a good film, your audience will be so caught up in the experience that any changes won't bother them.

One of the issues that came up early on was the question of how we were going to deal with the years between the time when Mike was a boy and when he becomes a young man. A novelist can simply write, "Time passed," and the job is done, but for screenwriters the situation is more difficult. The other thing a movie can't do is get inside Mike's head and show how Ben and Roundy's teachings were changing him, turning him into someone who would eventually refuse Ben's offer to lead the gang. Movies are always on the outside of their characters looking in. A writer, director, or actor can show *behavior* . . . but not *thought*.

So we decided to have Ben send Mike away to learn about the "real world." That way, Mike could return a different person (and an adult actor!), to see Ben Curry's hideout and the people there with fresh eyes . . . and it would allow the audience to see the situation in the same way. To heighten Mike's observable reactions, having him return as a sort of fish out of water seemed the best way to quickly show what had changed and how he had matured.

Another issue that came up while writing the treatment was that Dad's original idea of the Ben Curry gang pulling jobs all over the West, and then returning to their hideout in the Arizona Strip, was going to suck up a great deal of "story time." The long distances, which in reality would take many weeks to travel, had a tendency to kill the tension and the pacing in a movie version of the story.

Luckily, I still had my father to go to. I laid out the problem for him, asking what we could use as an alternative setting, an environment where the action could be a good deal more compact. He suggested setting the whole thing in the Gold Country of Northern California: After all, if you were an outlaw, you would have wanted to go where the money was.

I loved this idea. Just a few years earlier I had

worked on the CBS production of *The Shadow Riders,* which had used the beach areas of Santa Cruz, California, and then the rolling hills along the base of the Sierras near the town of Sonora as stand-ins for Texas. One of the things that bugged me about that movie, however, was the incredible lack of initiative some of the people involved had shown when it came to how they had used—or not used—this amazing locale. If a location wasn't specifically called for by the script, it tended to be ignored, no matter how much it might have contributed to the final look of the film!

As just one example, I remember driving to the set one day, a new location I had not seen before, with a pile of messages from the production office. When I arrived, I discovered the unit shooting a scene with Sam Elliott and Katharine Ross in some pools along the banks of the Stanislaus River. It was a nice-looking shot, but behind the lights and cameras was the Knight's Ferry Bridge. Built in 1863, it is the longest covered bridge west of the Mississippi. At one end were the remains of an 1854 flour mill, looking very much like bombed-out ruins appropriate for the end of the Civil War, and a stone house with barred windows. The production had discovered a unique use for the beautiful covered bridge: They had made it a shady cafeteria in which to serve lunch!

I cornered Verne Nobles, one of the producers and later a business partner of mine, and asked him what the hell was going on. Three fantastic-looking locations were just sitting there, and we had no plans to use any of them, not even to have the characters simply ride past. He sadly shook his head; I think he had been on the location scout, but he had been left out of the director's decisions on how to use the various places they had chosen. As a commercial artist and director of TV commercials, he was as befuddled by the waste of production value as I was.

So when considering new locations for *Son of a Wanted Man,* I was immediately intrigued by the idea of filming in all the wonderful places I had seen around Sonora. In addition to the locations I just described, there was also a railway with vintage engines and rolling stock, an 1890s roundhouse complete with vintage tools, quite a few old ranch buildings, and, best of all, the town of Columbia, which makes a brief appearance in *The Shadow Riders.* It is an actual town from the 1850s, and it has been preserved as a state park. The wonderful part is that these are not the interpretations of a Hollywood production designer or art director. It is all real! We attempted to include as many of these historical sites in our *Son of a Wanted Man* script as we could.

My father passed away in June 1988, and although we had a finished script, the whole project lay dormant for a while. Charlie got an acting job on *All My Children,* a soap opera shooting in New York, and headed to the East Coast. Eventually, I got a chance to send *Son of a Wanted Man* to a well-known cable TV channel. As has often been my experience over the years, the executives immediately turned around and tried to use my interest in making the one film as a lever to lock up the entire L'Amour estate. This was never going to happen. On top of that, after a certain amount of negotiating back and forth, it turned out they were also in the process of acquiring another of Dad's properties, one that we no longer controlled. Maybe they were planning on pitting one of us against the other, maybe they just wanted a fall-back position; I'm not sure. Discouraged by the roller coaster of emotions—not to mention the legal fees—associated with that whole adventure, I tossed the script in a drawer and headed off to do other things.

While he was in New York, Charlie went on to act in a number of the L'Amour Audio Dramas we were producing there, and he wrote quite a few of the scripts. For a while I was partnered with Verne Nobles, the producer from *The Shadow Riders*. We were able to get *The Iron Marshal*, retitled *Shaughnessy*, into production as a series pilot at CBS . . . but that project quickly turned into a disaster.

I doubt I can even remember all the things that went wrong. But just to demonstrate how even the best intentions, and the most talented people, can be wasted by the internal politics of the film and TV companies, allow me to list some of the people who worked on *Shaughnessy*. The screenplay was written by William Blinn, who started off working on shows like *Rawhide* and *Gunsmoke*. The middle of his career was marked by *Brian's Song, Starsky & Hutch,* and *Roots,* and he ended up helming *Eight Is Enough, Fame,* and *Pensacola* . . . quite a well-rounded résumé. One of the executive producers was Joel Fields, who has been a writer and producer on dozens of shows, including one of my favorites, *The Americans*. He is one of the best writers in the business.

Our line producer was the amazing Bernadette Caulfield, who in 2019 completed *Game of Thrones,* easily the greatest logistical challenge in the history of TV. Just looking at the supporting cast of *Shaughnessy* shows a group of seriously talented actors, including Sarah Paulson, John Carroll Lynch, John Hawkes, Bo Hopkins, Michael Jai White, and even Stuart Whitman, a Hollywood veteran of nearly fifty years. Many of the people the network turned down were also significantly talented, like Simon Baker, Hilary Swank, and Gretchen Mol. Our agent was Bettye McCartt, who managed Tom Selleck's career and was a major force behind Francis Ford Coppola's *The Godfather.*

When a film begins to go awry, the biggest issue is that generally there are a number of parties, all with differing agendas, who already have significant amounts of time and money involved. The only way to recoup those investments is to move forward. To slow the momentum of production is to risk its being canceled, a situation where everyone loses a good deal . . . and you never know if you're putting the brakes on something that might end up being a hit!

For better or for worse, Verne and I were able to use many of those great Northern California locations in *Shaughnessy.* The final result was not something I was the least bit proud of, but, as a learning experience, it had been invaluable. I had high hopes that I could quickly move on to producing *Son of a Wanted Man,* but after still more misadventures I realized it was simply not meant to be. Again the desk drawer beckoned, and again the project disappeared into darkness.

I REALLY LEARNED how to write, to improve my game to at least a somewhat professional level, while working on the Bantam series of Louis L'Amour Audio Dramas. It didn't hurt that I also had to shepherd other writers through the process, an aspect that made me think very carefully about what we were doing, and why. From the time I was a child, I tried to emulate my father, as well as many of the other adults around me. So of course I was always trying to create some story or other. Because I grew up on the periphery of Hollywood, the idea of making movies was an ever-present fantasy. I thought very little about the harsh realities of the business. What dreamer ever does?

I made Super 8 movies in junior high and high school, and 16-millimeter films in college, but it took me a long time to learn the fundamentals of the real craft of writing. Even now, to call myself a writer and to pretend that I exist at a level anywhere near many of those I hold in such high regard seems insufficiently humble! Mostly I make do and hope that multiple revisions, God, and the muse will all guide my hand.

For our purposes here, it is now important for me to rewind the clock slightly and mention two experiences from my last year at CalArts. Both of them did a lot to prepare me for writing projects to come, even though my role was that of director rather than a writer. In the first case, I shot a scene from a wonderfully written play by Sam Shepard. The other was a scene transcribed directly, word for word, from a Raymond Chandler short story. I had filmed short adaptations based on literary works before, but rather than using the author's own words, I had always adapted my own scripts, amateurish though they might have been. While the Shepard scene played as beautifully as you would expect from a Pulitzer Prize–winning playwright, the Chandler transcription was, as a piece of drama, a clunky mess. It quickly became obvious the reason for this was that it hadn't been specifically written to be *performed*. But until I improved my own writing skills, I couldn't completely understand all the ramifications of what that meant. I didn't understand, and I couldn't really begin to learn, until I studied acting.

Just as I wanted to write and direct, my sister dreamed of being an actor. She had been in school plays and such, but the process was a lot like the films I had made in school: They were merely practice at the crudest version of the art. She, however, found her way to taking a course with one of the greatest acting teachers of the last century, Sanford Meisner, and through him, she went on to study full-time with one of his best students, Janet Alhanti.

I could see the difference this training made in her work immediately. And eventually I began studying with Janet myself. I was never a particularly good student, and I was never a good actor. I never *wanted* to be a good actor. But I did learn what an actor requires from a writer in order to do the job. Slowly and painfully I learned how to structure scenes and design characters that would deliver the best performances.

When you write drama, the actors are the first consumer of your work, they are your true customers. Give them exactly what they need, and the scene will direct itself. People who write only novels and short stories rarely have any idea about how to do this . . . and to create literature, they shouldn't bother. Often what plays well as drama doesn't read very well at all.

Writing a good dialogue scene in a novel is a bit like giving the audience just the high points. Sometimes the words the characters speak are all there on the page, and sometimes they are not. Again, you make the reader your creative partner and let their imagination do some of the work. You can say things like "Jeffrey grumbled under his breath," and the reader doesn't have to know exactly what was said. In drama, though, not only do you have to write out every word, but it's better if you choose the specific words that will make the actor automatically grumble without even thinking about it. In literature, including every single bit of dialogue that could go into a scene is boring; it slows the pace of the narrative. In drama, the actor requires lines that build, systematically, from one emotional moment to the next, and therefore each and every reaction and line must be carefully crafted.

So I studied acting. I listened closely to my sister and her friends as they broke down each sentence of every role they auditioned for; this was how they knew exactly what they needed to do with every line and moment. Using those same techniques, I started trying to write in a way that made the intention of the scenes and the lines I was creating clear . . . at least to a well-trained actor.

IT WAS JUST a little bit before this time that Bantam Books had come to my father and asked him if they could use his material to experiment with a new medium they were considering: audiobooks. Now, the idea of selling recordings of people reading novels and poetry and things like that dates back to the 1930s or before. For a long time, the majority of these recordings, including some of Dad's titles, were produced and distributed by the National Library Service's Books for the Blind program. Eventually, some specialty publishers like Caedmon Records, Listening Library, and Books on Tape built themselves a niche, offering a somewhat more commercial version of the same thing.

In the mid-1980s, however, the major book publishers noticed that while reading had declined, the time people spent commuting had significantly increased. Some smart executive put two and two together and realized those hours spent on the road were an opportunity the mainstream publishing industry could attempt to exploit. In a very short time, most of the big publishers began to develop audio publishing arms.

In order to test the market, Bantam chose its most consistently popular author, my father. In addition to normal bookstores, the publisher also planned special displays in a venue that seemed like a slam dunk for his audience: truck stops. The targets were not only the professional drivers who spent their lives staring into an infinity of taillights and asphalt, but also commuters and even vacation drivers, particularly families, who enjoyed the very country that Louis wrote about.

The newly formed Bantam Audio Publishing division was very cautious in its approach. The team asked to produce a series of recordings of Dad's Western short stories. They specifically wanted something that would fit on a single sixty-minute cassette, which they could sell for a reasonable amount of money. An unabridged novel might run six to twelve hours or more, and they were rightly concerned that the correspondingly high prices might sabotage the market for audiobooks before it even got established.

Dad pushed back. He was concerned that many of his early pulp magazine stories, particularly the Chick Bowdrie, Texas Ranger, series that was being proposed, were not really good enough and might be too dated for the audience. He felt some additional aspect was needed. In a series of discussions held over a couple of days at our ranch in Colorado, a decision was finally made. Bantam would go ahead with the Bowdrie stories, but they would be dramatized, like the classic radio dramas produced between the 1920s and the 1950s, in order to offer what Dad hoped would be additional production value. They would also experiment with the "single voice" or "narrator" style of production using some of the short stories that Dad thought were better quality, like those from his collection *Yondering*.

A producer and director, David Rapkin and Charles Potter, were hired, and a prototype story, "Strange Pursuit," was produced. Some of the production techniques were then refined, and it was followed by "A Trail to the West" and "Where Buzzards Fly." Each of these stories became shows that featured a cast of actors playing the individual roles, a narrator, sound effects, and music. And they contained an additional recording of my father discussing various aspects of the story.

It was right around this point when I came up for air after that job in TV at Finnegan Associates. After hearing the first couple of productions, Dad had begun having reservations about the new audio dramas, and since I had some background in production, scriptwriting, acting, and sound recording, he thought I was the perfect person to look into it. I was also out of work, and he may have thought it best to promptly put my nose back into contact with the grindstone.

His primary concern was that "the actors weren't very good." I put that in quotes not just because it's what Dad said, but because, as we will later see, it wasn't really the case at all. The other thing that had him worried was the time it took to record his own commentary, the material that filled out the additional minutes left on many of the early audiobooks. Dad felt he was "log rolling," just riffing on and on without a real goal in mind. He was concerned that he might get to a point where he was repeating himself and that he was wasting time in which he could be writing new material.

So I started going with Dad to the recording sessions and interviewing him in order to keep his responses organized and fresh. This wasn't a long-term solution, but it was something we could do right away. I also made him prepare the material the day before. Dad was very good at reading aloud, so it was easy for him to work from a script, especially one he had written. The results were a significant improvement, but I'm not sure he liked this approach any better than the "make it up as you go along" plan Bantam had started him off with. It wasn't just that it was an interruption; it was that he had to keep to *their* schedule, rather than doing it at his own pace and on his own time.

The question about acting quality was one that I approached very cautiously. I didn't know the first thing about what David Rapkin and Charles Potter were doing in New York. So I began traveling east to observe their productions, particularly the auditions. It didn't take long to realize that there was nothing wrong with the actors. Everyone who came through the process was a professional. Many spent their days doing radio and TV ads or parts on soap operas and often wrapping up the evening by playing roles on Broadway. For example, the narrator for the Chick Bowdrie stories was playing the lead in *Phantom of the Opera* at the same time as working for us. And, as a younger man, Academy Award winner J. K. Simmons auditioned for a number of parts in our audio dramas and performed in at least one of them.

Yet Dad *still* didn't like the performances, and I agreed with him. They were acceptable at a certain level, but they could have been a good deal better. I was pretty sure I'd discovered what was wrong, and if I was correct, my solution would also spare Dad the interruptions he disliked so much, when he was hustled off to the recording studio every other month to record more additional material.

THE PROBLEM RELATED back to the two projects I had directed near the end of my time at CalArts, the play by Sam Shepard and the scene from the short story by Raymond Chandler. The lesson that I had accidently learned was that *literature* is definitely not *drama.* The scripts for the early Louis L'Amour Audio Dramas were simply transcribed, word for word, from his short stories. All description was read by the narrator. The dialogue was read by the various actors. No other changes were made. If Dad expected the performances to improve, then the shows were going to have to be *adapted,* just like a movie, by people who knew how to write drama. At its fundamental level, the difference between literature and audio drama couldn't be clearer. One is created to be seen, a visual medium, even if it is just letters on a page; the other is designed to be heard.

Dad was already very alert to the visual aspect of writing and reading, often lecturing young writers on the advantages of artfully breaking up their paragraphs so "the eye could rest," and how it was often best to say less rather than more in the process of telling your story. To put it into modern terms, the words and letters in our language are code, like a vastly more complex version of computer code, and the reader's brain is the processor. This turns the active imagination of the reader into the greatest asset of the writer. Reader and writer become partners in the creative experience: The writer's job is to inspire the reader's imagination to create a "personal best" version of the story.

However, as an increasing amount of that "processing" or imagination is handed over to the artists involved in an audio drama, TV show, film, stage play, or comic book, more careful and artful adaptation needs to be done to make it all acceptable to the audience. The bottom line is, if you want good actors to do a good job, you can't give them just a few lines from a short story; you have to give them truly well-constructed scenes for them to sink their teeth into. Not many writers of literature attempt to construct complete scenes like a dramatist; the scenes may play well when listened to, but they don't read well at all.

Hiring writers well versed in drama to adapt the stories would have an additional upside. Through the adaptation process, the scripts could be made exactly as long as Bantam needed them to be. One of the things I had discovered was that while the people at Bantam Audio Publishing had gone to great lengths to pick stories that would end up being as close to the required sixty minutes as possible, they were expecting my father, with his introductions or "commentary," to fill up the remaining time. This was a problem for a couple of reasons. They were rapidly running out of stories that were approximately the right length, and they had never told Dad the program was going to require his time continually! The whole process was so new that they had never really planned for ongoing success.

Having each of the cassette tapes—and later, CDs—be a minimum of sixty minutes was very important to the publishing team because they were convinced that the consumer compared prices based on the overall length of the program. If they charged too much money for too few minutes, the audience would feel ripped off. On the other hand, if a program ran too long, that was time not included in the price and thus the company would lose money. I have no idea if all this was true, but they were sure getting the balance right was critical . . . and I was sure that adapting the stories would fix the problem.

Once a writer starts interpreting the story for a new medium, a great deal of flexibility is possible. I think the shortest story I personally adapted to the 60-minute format was "The One for the Mojave Kid," which was around ten pages. Later, I adapted "The Diamond of Jeru," which started as an unpublished twelve-page short story, into an eighty-page novella (published in *Off the Mangrove Coast*), then a 90-minute TV movie and, eventually, an audio drama that ran 180 minutes. I wouldn't have believed it when I started, but somehow that story had an incredible amount of potential to look ever more deeply into itself. Adaptation is the process of stripping a story down to its essence, which often means giving up on some of your favorite moments, and then building it back up using just the elements that support the drama. You can usually fit all sorts of information back in as you discover how the scenes will play, but it is more in the form of characterization and nuance.

However, back in the days when we started, I knew such things only vaguely. And I was faced with the problem of having to hire writers who, no doubt, had done more work than I had and possibly knew more than I did . . . or at least they might think so. I realized I was going to need an example, something that showed I understood what I was talking about. In fact, I was faced with a more serious situation even than that. I was going to have to go out and create a show that forced me to learn everything I would need to know in order to teach our audio writers what was going to be required.

So with a group of friends, people I knew from school and from working on various student films, I wrote and directed a production based on Dad's noir thriller "Unguarded Moment." Paul O'Dell, the producer and editor, I had known since my early teens in Durango, Colorado. Roy Parsons, the engineer, and I had gone to CalArts together. Fred Paroutaud was a fellow car enthusiast and had written an incredible music score for a student film I'd made. And John Putch, who played the lead, was someone I had gone to high school with, and we had made Super 8 movies together.

I'm still quite fond of the writing, and the actors' performances, in "Unguarded Moment," even though the technical aspects of the production leave an awful lot to be desired. That's not surprising: We didn't yet know what we were doing, and we were working on borrowed equipment and a threadbare budget. But it did prove that I was headed in the right direction when it came to delivering better performances through the adaptation process. I also learned a great deal, and that gave me the confidence to push forward and work with other writers.

The first person I hired was a man named Bill Whitehead, a family friend who had written episodes of a number of popular TV shows. Bill was incredibly patient as I tried to figure out the parameters for writing the Louis L'Amour audio dramas and how I would get the sort of results I desired, not just from myself but from others.

A year or so after my father died, I wrote and directed another production, "Merrano of the Dry Country." It was an attempt at producing a different style of show, grittier and more realistic, and pushing the quality of the acting to an even higher level. Dad had tried to write a Western with both a racial and an ecological angle, an interesting move for 1948, and I wanted to add to that, doing something that was hard-hitting, raw, and emotional.

By the time of "Merrano," our technical standards had improved considerably, as had our abilities, even though Paul and I were still educating ourselves as we went along. I was constantly reading technical articles and textbooks and talking to as many engineers as I could find. Unlike when we did "Unguarded Moment," we finally had some of our own equipment, and we received the regular Bantam Audio production budget. Both "Unguarded Moment" and "Merrano" were cut and mixed on tape, but I was already trying to teach myself about the brand-new digital equipment. While we were still editing, we met Howard Gale, a veteran engineer, whose help on the technical side would prove invaluable when it came to the final mix. With Howard's input, we developed a number of innovative techniques for recording and mixing in stereo, techniques that we are still using (and are still innovative) even thirty years later.

Because we constantly needed writers, the L'Amour series of audio dramas brought in people from all sorts of places, like students from UCLA and interns from the Los Angeles Theatre Center. The most prolific of our scribes were Katherine Nolan (who also worked on the *Law of the Desert Born* graphic novel) and Charles Van Eman, with whom, you will remember, I had written the *Son of a Wanted Man* screenplay. Charlie and Katherine each adapted seven of the L'Amour audios, a tie for the record.

For quite a few years our audio dramas were also broadcast on the radio. We had a syndicate of more than two hundred stations, in addition to Armed Forces Radio. My crew in Los Angeles, Paul O'Dell and Howard Gale, recut and remastered the shows so that they could go out in a format appropriate for all the various stations.

As time passed, however, the audio publishing industry became fully mature. The audience was more and more willing to pay for much longer, single-voice readings. The need to produce odd, attention-grabbing ideas, like dramatized short stories, became a thing

of the past. In the early days, nearly every audio publisher experimented with creating dramas. But eventually, most of them had given up. We had been one
of the first, and we ended up being one of the last.

A critical aspect to maintaining a relationship with
any publisher is to be attentive to their need to make
a profit. So finally I had to tell them it was time to
start producing the L'Amour novels as unabridged
readings, the same as everybody else in the business.
It was a bittersweet decision because I knew it would,
sooner or later, bring the production of the dramas to
a close. The profit potential in the single-voice, unabridged readings was significantly greater.

In the late 1990s the New York productions of the
dramas begin to wind down. In fact, Charlie Van
Eman's last script, "Alkali Basin," was never even recorded. Most of the crew, both in New York and Los
Angeles, went off in various directions . . . all but
David Rapkin. He remained, faithfully producing the
L'Amour unabridged audiobooks that were being
brought out by what was, by this time, Random
House Audio Publishing. On the positive side, it
turned out my instincts had been right: The single-
voice readings sold exceptionally well and, as of
2023, David is still producing a few more every year.

THIS RAMBLING HISTORY of audio publishing rejoins
the story of *Son of a Wanted Man* around 1998. It
was then that Charlie Van Eman and I went on a
long, crazy road trip, up through California to Wash-

ington, east through the Dakotas to Minnesota, then south to the Texas coast and home to Southern California by way of the L'Amour ranch in Colorado. We wanted to stop in as many of the places that my Dad had visited on his travels as possible. At some point in our eleven-thousand-mile drive, we ended up discussing a film that had come out a year or two earlier, *Shakespeare in Love.* Not only had it been wonderfully written and quite funny, but the script had a lot of insight into the pitfalls of making theater—or movies, audio dramas, or any other kind of scripted performance.

There is a critical moment when a young William Shakespeare has had his theater closed by the Powers That Be. In this case, that power is the bureaucrat in charge of public entertainment, but it just as easily could have been a movie studio turning down a script or canceling the preparations to make a movie. In *Shakespeare in Love,* Richard Burbage, the man in charge of a rival theater company, decides the honorable thing to do is to offer a solution to his would-be enemy, Shakespeare. His line is a classic: "The Master of the Revels despises us all for vagrants and peddlers of bombast. But my father, James Burbage, had the first license to make a company of players from Her Majesty, and he drew from poets, the literature of the age. We must show them that we are men of parts. Will Shakespeare has a play. I have a theater. The Curtain [Burbage's theater] is yours."

I thought of the various struggles I'd been involved with in trying to get movies made, and also of the lucky breaks that had allowed me to hang on to the rights to the *Son of a Wanted Man* screenplay, rather than having them lost in a blizzard of competing contracts. "You know, Charlie," I said, "*we* are 'men of parts,' "—meaning actors and writers and such. "I'm going to find a way to make our script, and we're going do it without the sort of compromises that every production company tried to force down our throats." Of course, I was thinking of producing it as an audio drama, but that program was almost at its end, and none of us had ever done a production that would be as long, complex, or expensive as our movie script. It took over year for the right opportunity to present itself.

With the turn of the century, a new force came into our lives: the Louis L'Amour website, louislamour.com. The critical aspect, that opportunity I mentioned, for the next chapter in the life of *Son of a Wanted Man* was that our webmaster was my old friend Paul O'Dell. With him on salary, there just might be a chance to do one more production, a novel, a nice high point on which to end the audio drama program.

There are lots of different ways of putting an audio drama together. Some think the only way is to produce them "live," a complex process of having the actors, the narrator (if there is one), sound effects, and even the musicians all in the studio at the same time in order to create the show in a single pass . . . produced like a piece of theater, or a classic-era radio production. When I had first started working with David Rapkin and Charles Potter, they had wisely chosen a modification of this approach. Each scene was produced in radio-drama style, with all the actors, the narrator, and a sound-effects man all in the studio doing their thing together. But by leaving the music and some other sound effects until later, Rapkin and Potter could still do multiple takes and retain some capacity to edit those takes in postproduction.

I find both of these approaches a bit overwhelming. I've never been able to concentrate on all the details of a scene simultaneously and then bring them together with the perfect timing required to do a truly good job . . . and to try and produce an entire show in one pass is definitely outside of my skill set!

My training in audio production has all been centered around the film business, where everything is assembled in separate pieces, each of which can be adjusted as needed, all the way until the final mix. This was the approach Paul and I used on the audio dramas I had written and directed in Los Angeles. The problem with the "movie method" was that it took a long time to carefully select the best performance for each actor in every scene, then lay in the sound effects and music, and mix it all together. Although the greatest amount of money always went to the cast, the greatest amount of time was spent editing and mixing. *Son of a Wanted Man* was going to be a big show, and I didn't want to simply do a longer version of what we had done in the past. If we couldn't shoot for the next level of quality, it wasn't going to be worth our time or energy. And with Paul on the Louis L'Amour payroll, we just might be able to afford the postproduction time we would need to pull it off.

The first challenge was the script. It was in good shape where the scenes were concerned, but it was going to need narration. In addition, there should be a dialogue scene right up front, to be sure the audience knew they were listening to a drama and not a single-voice reading. While creating this beginning I came up with the idea of having the narrator speak in the sort of language found in nineteenth-century literature. And he would give the audience a pair of historical "bookends" to the story. This would introduce some of the history of the California gold rush in the beginning, and then, for the end, would conclude the story of Ben Curry, bringing it up into the twentieth century. Wrapping up the story in that way was a mechanism Dad had used very effectively in *Dark Canyon* and a couple of other novels. I always found it to be a wonderful, and oddly emotional, way to conclude a story.

As I dived deeper into writing the narration, and also breaking down the intention behind every line of the script so that I could direct the actors, I began to notice some hidden details that I could work with. Some were just notes related to what I wanted from the performances, but others inspired significant rewrites. Here are several examples. . . .

Mike has three fathers: his real father (who is killed early on), Ben Curry, and also Roundy. All contribute to who he becomes. He is interesting because he is eventually able to discover the best in each of them and incorporate that into his life.

From the first draft of the script, Ben was always a charming and deadly sociopath, a man with a sense of honor but little conscience. But an additional quality of Ben's that appeared later was that of a little boy who had never grown up, who was still playing at being an outlaw and had a romantic vision of himself in that role. It comes out in many ways, but at one point in the script he says, "I thought I was 'Brennan on the Moor' or perhaps Robin Hood. Only I gave mine to the poor saloonkeepers and the ladies of—well, let's just say the ladies."

Although Ben is a good-enough parent to send Mike away to learn about the real world, he then makes the mistake of entertaining himself with another surrogate son, the outlaw Kirby Perrin. This is played mostly in subtext, thus giving the actors something to work with, but it gives the rivalry that Perrin feels between himself and Mike, and his relationship with Ben, some added depth. This is the sort of thing that I like to discover in an adaptation, adding an extra touch of detail to the original material . . . the sort of touch that specifically enhances the relationships in a dramatized production.

A big influence on some of these last-minute changes in Ben was that I had decided I was going to cast Will MacMillan, who had played the "heavy," Joe Stangle, in "Merrano of the Dry Country." Though he was a very lighthearted soul, Will had made a career out of playing a string of smaller "bad guy" roles in movies like *Dirty Harry* and *Salvador.* I thought it would be wonderful to give him a big, complex, leading-man part. He was also the sort of actor who could really deliver the goods when it came to subtle emotion.

Many of his performances in individual takes often seemed all over the place, but if you were patient enough to let him do it a few times, he would always give you all the raw material you needed to cut together a really terrific performance. Years later, when we were doing our audio adaptation of "The Diamond of Jeru," a young lady who was a newcomer to our process watched him performing a small part. She shook her head and said, "What's up with this guy?" Paul and I just grinned at each other. "Just wait till we get his tracks into the editing room," we told her. "You'll eat your words."

Casting the part of Mike also created some changes in the script. I was considering a young guy in my acting class named George Perez. He had immigrated from Mexico not long after he was born, but he still had a very slight Spanish accent. I'd heard him control it during scenes in class, but in audio accents are pure gold: In a medium that has no pictures, they are a great way of differentiating one actor from another. The more I thought about George playing the part, the more I liked the idea of "Mike" being Latino. It showed that Ben had an open mind, no prejudice, yet it also allowed Mike to always feel like a bit of an outsider among the members of the gang . . . and thus to want to be accepted even more. Was he his real father's son, Ben's son, Roundy's son . . . or his own man? That's the dilemma Mike must solve in order to have an adult relationship with Ben. The other thing that made me doubly happy to hire George was that he had a nephew who had actually played a younger version of him in another production! Thus Mike

Bastian from the novel became Mike Santos in the audio.

Casting is full of interesting trade-offs. Later on, when we held auditions for "The Diamond of Jeru" audio drama, there were two equally great pairs of actors to play John and Helen Lacklan, the married couple who are a major aspect of that story. But you couldn't mix and match the two Johns with the two Helens . . . once you did, they were no longer believable as a married couple.

Or sometimes there is a great actor for a certain part, but they sound too much like another actor who has already been cast. You have to make a lot of choices that have nothing to do with talent, and none of them are easy.

Casting is exhausting if you have to start from scratch, so for *Son of a Wanted Man,* I took as many people as I could from Janet Alhanti's acting class and filled in many of the other parts with their friends and acquaintances. Some of them had been around the business for ages; others were newcomers. J. G. Hertzler (Roundy) had been working in Hollywood for thirty years; among other things, he had played a staggering eight different roles in the Star Trek franchise, and he then went on to teach acting at Cornell. Lee Reherman (Perrin) actually played football for Cornell and graduated with an MBA. He was working on his doctorate in economics at UCLA while acting on the side. In the midst of all this, he also competed on the *American Gladiators* TV show and played a number of small parts in TV and film. Burr DeBenning (Colley) had dozens of credits, including

TV Westerns like *Iron Horse, Custer, The Outcasts, Lancer, The Virginian, Bonanza,* and *Daniel Boone.* Jason Corbett (the Marshal) also had a fair number of TV credits and appeared in a local country-and-western band. Oddly, two of our cast members had once been lawyers: Bob Glouberman, who has a long résumé of various character roles, and Deirdre Delaney Gurney (Drusilla), who, though a fine actress, eventually joined her husband on the production side of the business, producing shows like *Duck Dynasty* and events such as Shark Week.

Charlie Van Eman was co-producer with Paul O'Dell, as well as playing the part of outlaw gang member Frank. And when Fred Paroutaud married and moved away and we needed a new composer, Charlie introduced us to John Philip Shenale. "Phil," as we call him, had worked with musicians like Tori Amos, Diana Ross, Rick Springfield, John Hiatt, and the Beach Boys. Nicholas Ballas, an old friend from college and a reliable source of help and advice, also joined the cast, as Joaquin Molina. The one thing we try to do above and beyond everything else is to hire interesting people, and people who, even if they aren't friends, are the sort of people we would enjoy spending time with. Life is too short and the pay is too low to put up with jerks!

Recording the actors' voices took about five days. For the best sound quality, I like to work in a large studio, the kind designed for orchestras. Our actors don't wear headphones and are not isolated from one another in voice-over booths. I want to keep their interaction as natural as possible.

The more I've done this, the more relaxed I've become about actors not being perfectly "on mic." Most of the scenes in *Son of a Wanted Man* were recorded with the actors standing in front of their microphones and reading their lines off of scripts set on music stands, but whenever it was necessary to get the right sound, we would have them move around a bit or follow them with a mic on a boom (a long pole) as if we were recording a movie.

Some actors really create their performance out of physical movement, and you restrict that at your peril. George Perez, who had also trained as a dancer, was always best when he was moving. In the scene when he crosses the wire bridge that is Ben's secret way across the river, we made him balance on the narrow edge of a two-by-four, and often in between takes he would simply jump up and down to keep his performance from getting "frozen" at the microphone. Since he worked all day for most of the schedule, this was probably exhausting!

We bring a lot of props to the studio—in this case, a saddle for actors to lift when saddling horses, the two-by-fours, some poles that could double for guns or tools, and several solid chairs that wouldn't make noise when the actors climbed onto or jumped off of them.

I record a lot of takes, which gives Paul a great deal of variety in the editing process. Whether you like it or not, each take is always subtly different, and the best scenes are often constructed by combining the material from several. We'll record the whole scene, carefully sticking to the script, and then break it down and work just with the individual pages or lines. Toward the end of the time allotted for a scene, we will often do careful improvisations. Sometimes changing a few words is a better way to direct a performance than asking the actor to accomplish something different with their reading of a line. Occasionally, I will jump in and work with an actor, playing the other part in a scene. As I mentioned, I'm not a very good actor, but I know enough to alter my performance in order to get the reaction I want from someone who is more talented than I am.

In the early days, I tried to direct from inside the control room, but by the time we recorded *Son of a Wanted Man,* I was spending all my time in the studio with the actors. It was disruptive to come barging into the actor's space every time I had a note. "What did I do wrong now?" they would wonder. Paul had operations in the control room well in hand, and if I simply remained in the studio, then directing the actors was a bit like a calm and uninterrupted exploration of what we wanted the scenes to become . . . very much like a rehearsal.

ONCE THE PROCESS of recording the actor's voices was finished, we could relax. From that point on, it was just Paul and I, and we could work on our own schedule . . . and on *Son of a Wanted Man,* we *had* to work on our own schedule. The only way we could afford the lengthy process of editing and mixing was to do it in our spare time.

Paul was still busy building the website, and I was

editing several books of short stories, so after a break to catch up on all this other work, we began editing the dialogue tracks. All the different takes of each scene were compared, and then each line was assembled to produce the best performance. It's not only the most convincing performance of a line that makes the difference; very often, timing is a significant component. A good editor can add or subtract that half second that suggests arrogance or a lack of confidence, impatience or careful thought. Sometimes emphasis can be supplied by subtly increasing the volume on a key word or by searching out where the actor used that same word in another scene and using that alternative version. It took a total of about nine weeks to cut the dialogue, but given our other obligations, we were able to fit in only about one week of work a month.

It was right around this time when a good friend, movie producer Michael Joyce, asked me if I wanted to sell one of Dad's adventure stories to USA Network. Very generously, he also offered me the chance to produce it with him. We chose "The Diamond of Jeru," but as the contract negotiations drew to a close, I began to feel like I would really like to write the script as well. This was vastly easier said than done; studios are quite reluctant to hire a writer who is not on one of their exclusive "lists." Well, I hadn't worked in the film business in eight years or so. I wasn't on anybody's list, and I certainly wasn't going to be invited. However, a strange and fortuitous alignment of the stars had begun.

First was the fact that Hollywood always shuts

down for a month or more around the holidays, and
it was already after Thanksgiving. Second, both the
Writers Guild and the Screen Actors Guild had contracts that were up for renegotiation over the coming
summer. That meant the film would need to be finished by then, or the production would run the risk
of being stalled by a strike. Moreover, if our production had to wait until after the new contracts were
signed, a process that might take many months, the
film faced a serious chance of being canceled. The
creative executives who run things in the TV world
are constantly on the move, being fired, edging up the
corporate ladder, or quitting to pursue less stressful
jobs. Few creative executives want to put a film se-
lected by their predecessor into production. If it's successful they don't really get the credit, and if it's a
failure they will certainly take the blame. If there was
a change in executives before it went into production, our project would probably be as good as dead.

So it was in everyone's interest to move quickly . . .
after the holidays, that is. As I thought about it, I realized that I had until the middle of January to write
a script. If I was able to create something acceptable,
it would be very difficult for them to turn it down
because we would have a good shot at finishing before any possible strikes. On the other hand, if they
did turn it down, I would have to produce the film
with the discredit of that failure hanging over my
head. There are trade-offs to everything.

I began writing like a madman. Much of the time
Paul and I were editing *Son of a Wanted Man*, I was
also scribbling away, roughing out scenes that I

would then stay up past midnight typing into a more polished form. My gamble paid off, and even though there eventually *was* a change in executives at USA Network, we were close enough to our start date to survive it. We finalized the dialogue editing on *Son of a Wanted Man* in February, and by early March, I was headed to Australia to start preproduction on the film adaptation of "The Diamond of Jeru."

When I got back in July, Paul and I threw ourselves into the next stage of postproduction on *Son of a Wanted Man*. This meant going on the road to create the sound effects, and it is probably the most fun aspect of the entire process. I had gone to the trouble of installing a high-quality battery power supply into the camper area of my Dodge pickup truck. Using that, we could bring a case of equipment from our recording studio into the field. The camper wasn't very big or warm (we do a lot of our recording in the winter because there isn't as much noise from birds and creeks, and there is little danger of fire), and we couldn't record very far away from the truck, but we made it work.

Getting out into nature, being able to break furniture, set fires, shoot guns, fall down, run around, and generally act like eight-year-olds—all while pretending to be doing it for professional reasons—is a blast. At the same time, it is all managed for safety, and every bit of material we record is carefully logged. While Paul runs the recorder, I create nearly every sound effect: every footstep, squeak of saddle leather, or strike of a match.

The worst effects are the body falls, like when

someone hits the ground when they are shot or punched or knocked off a horse. That is actually me falling onto whatever surface is needed: wood floor, hard-packed dirt, or ice-cold water. Using padding just doesn't sound right, and doing it is definitely the sort of thing that reminds you of your age. Recording all the footsteps (except the women; we try to hire an actress for that) on a wide variety of surfaces is time-consuming, exacting, and extremely boring. Every time there is a plane in the sky or a car on a distant road, we stop and wait for silence. Recording props and animals is a good deal more amusing. We rented a real stagecoach with a team of four, and a friend of ours who is a rodeo champion showed up with his best horse and created a lot of effects for us. We even recorded the "breaking" of a newly trained pony, the very first time she was ridden. That was rather dramatic!

We created some very distinctive firearms effects for the show. Technically, the most interesting may have been either a 375-yard shot into a frozen turkey (thank you very much), so that we could separate the sound of the bullet's impact from the crack of the rifle, or a long-range shot with a big-bore (.60-caliber) muzzle loader where we used a very light powder charge in an attempt to record the ball whooshing past the microphones. That worked pretty well, but we still had to slow the effect down further in post-production. Additionally, we had the opportunity to shoot up an old cabin that was about to be demolished. It was safely down in a small hollow, and we placed our microphones inside, marking where they were on the outer walls with spray paint. Then we methodically shot through the walls and glass. When Ben Curry is trapped inside his house by the outlaw gang, what you hear is the actual sound of bullets penetrating the wood planks and windows. I was even able to get the sound of one lightly loaded pistol ball bouncing around the interior and then rolling to a stop. It was only later that we discovered that some of the best bullet hits and ricochets can be obtained in a less dramatic manner by using a Wrist-Rocket slingshot and ball bearings or oddly shaped pebbles. Both Paul and I have been pretty well trained in safely executing these minor pyrotechnics while working on a number of movies . . . so if you're an amateur, please don't try any of this stuff at home!

It is worth noting that when you see Western movies and one character breaks a chair over another's head, the result is totally unrealistic. We tried it, hitting a carpet-covered sawhorse with an old wooden chair that we had weakened by taking it apart and putting it loosely back together . . . and it *still* nearly ripped my arms off. The geometry of a chair is extraordinarily strong! It took several swings before it broke, and I was vibrating like a cartoon character by the time we were done.

All in all, the most important "prop" for recording our sound effects has been the L'Amour family ranch in Colorado. With several small houses that could be used for doors and floors, as well as the barns, workshops, horses, dogs, gates, and old tools, plus having the guys who work there to help us out, we had nearly everything we needed. We also had wonderfully quiet open spaces in which to record ambience: the elements, the wind, thunder, birds, crickets, and frogs that set the stage for, and became background to, every scene. As the ranch is located near Durango, Colorado, we also had access to the narrow-gauge railway there and its steam locomotives. Additionally, we did a fair amount of recording around Sonora, California, the area where we had once planned on shooting the movie version of the story. There is something distinctive about the sound of California's wilderness, and we wanted to add that to the overall effect.

After several "recording safaris" we had hours of sound effects in the can, and it was time to begin cutting them into the show. This is the point where the final timing for each scene starts to come together. Before the sound effects are edited, however, I sit down and record a rough track of the narration. I like to put off recording the actual narrator as long as possible. If you need to remove a scene, or adjust any other aspect of the show, being able to rewrite the narration is a great way to make a seamless change. At the same time, it's impossible to edit the sound effects into a scene, and get the timing right, without the narration included . . . so I do a temporary version.

Having to read my own writing is a very good test of how much I like the narration, and I often rewrite it as we are recording to make it sound better or to be less confusing. It's also useful because it shows the actor who eventually reads the narration that you have also done the work. Actors are constantly convinced that directors don't understand or appreciate what they do. To that end, it is worth noting that doing narration is *hard*. I am terrible at it, and I have high expectations for myself, even though no one will hear my work. I find it completely exhausting, and I know I could never do it for a living!

Once the temporary narration is recorded, we begin laying it into the scenes along with the sound effects. Many more adjustments are made because often just the strategically placed sound of feet moving slightly on the floor or a character shifting his weight in a chair can greatly improve a performance. This is the really exciting part of the editing process because it's the first moment where what we are doing begins to sound like the finished show.

Throughout postproduction we are always trying to figure out who our narrator is going to be. In the case of *Son of a Wanted Man*, we went back through many of the people who had done the single-voice readings of Dad's novels and short stories to remind ourselves of who we liked and why. Every time we found someone we thought might be good, we cut some of their material into our show to see how it sounded alongside our cast members. Because it came from another story, the narration itself generally made no sense, but it did give us an idea of whether the voices blended well.

The best fit by far was Terrence Mann, a Broadway veteran (and more recently seen in the Apple TV+ adaptation of Isaac Asimov's *Foundation* series) who had also done a bang-up job reading our *Beyond the Great Snow Mountains* short-story collection. Specifically, he had given each of the stories a slightly different interpretation, the sign of someone who is a real artist. And just to prove that the world of the theater is very small indeed, later on I found myself doing some work with his father-in-law, the great ballet dancer and choreographer Jacques d'Amboise!

Terrence was based in New York, so I had to fly there to record his tracks. At this point, David Rapkin was good enough to step in to produce and prepare the session for me. Our time was limited: Terrence was just finishing up as one of the leads in some big show—it might have been *Les Misérables*—and he was a new father as well. It was kind of like old times to be recording in Manhattan again, even if it was only for a couple of days.

Once Terry's work was cut into the scenes and another round of adjustments had been made, it was time for our composer to take over. Sitting down with Phil Shenale, we "spotted" the show, marking the points where music might fade in and out on a script. Unlike a movie, where the timing of everything is forcefully determined by the picture, an audio drama has the advantage of giving the composer some flexibility. If the music needed another couple of seconds, a slightly different sound-effects mix, or a modified ending to a scene, we were happy to oblige.

Phil used a variety of wonderful instruments. First and foremost was a piano frame, which had been removed from the piano and was then played with hammers, almost like a weird combination of a harp and a xylophone. He also used a century-old Marxophone, a zitherlike instrument that he may have learned to use while working with the Beach Boys, and a Chamberlin, an odd keyboard from the early 1950s that uses tape loops to make it almost like an early analog sampler. Phil's Chamberlin looked like it had been rescued from the wreck of the *Titanic* with a chainsaw, and its sound became more and more interesting as it neared the point where it seemed ready to completely fall apart.

Instead of having a composer deliver finished music files, we prefer to mix every instrument in the score ourselves. That way, we can carefully work in and around where we have placed all of our other sounds. When we get ready to do a final mix, we always consult with a wonderful colleague of ours named Ken Goerres. Ken has mixed a good many albums and concerts, but I believe the discipline that has made him so helpful to our projects is that he is a top-end speaker designer. Many engineers can discover the right equalization, the tonal balance, for a voice or instrument by adjusting the controls up and down to find the sweet spot. Ken just sits in the back of the studio and calls out stuff like "Minus three decibels at 250 hertz." I don't know how he does it, but he's nearly always right!

In this last phase, a lot of fussy adjustments are made. We have to be sure the show sounds good on most systems, not just in our studio. Many of our listeners are in cars, so it has to work in small spaces and with road noise in the background. At the same time, we don't want to lose all the delicate qualities we worked so hard to record, and we want it to sound good in a living room too. Every one of these choices is a compromise: For everything you gain, you have to give up something somewhere. Over the years I have never listened to one of my shows without wanting to make some changes, without wishing I knew more about how to do a better job.

When we started production on *Son of a Wanted Man,* I got in touch with a top supervising sound editor for motion pictures, a guy who was well known for taking responsibility for the entire sound production process, from the tracks that are recorded on set all the way through to the delivery of the pieces that could eventually be used to create foreign language dubs; there are very few who bother to stick with the process in order to manage all these details. I asked him if he had ever mixed a show entirely "in the box," meaning digitally, completely inside a computer program, rather than going through the sort of giant mixing consoles typically found at movie studios. He said no, and that he didn't know anyone else who had either. "Well, we're doing it," I told him. He was very excited by the idea and, possibly with some skepticism, wished us luck.

Because *Son of a Wanted Man* took about four years to produce, I'm not sure if we ended up being the very first production to do an "in the box" mix. At around one hundred tracks, our mix wasn't as complex as most feature films, but it was easily as large as many TV movies. I think what I can say is that we were *one* of the first, and we proved it could be done—to ourselves, if no one else. Looking back after twenty years, I find it laughable that whether or not you could do a mix inside a computer was even a question. What was then an experimental process is now done many times a day.

The last piece of the production was cutting together an interview with my father, mostly from material that had been recorded by an old friend, Mike Pizzuto, for a documentary when we were in college. That and a "making of" bonus piece filled up the required 180 minutes, or three audio CDs. In a strange way, we had come full circle, back to the time when my father had added his voice to the earliest of the audio dramas to make the length turn out correct.

I had planned on *Son of a Wanted Man* being the last of our audio dramas. We tried to outdo everything we had done before and go out on a high note. We were relatively successful. We're not as talented as a lot of people working in film, but we don't do it every day, and we've had to learn nearly everything on our own. In general, I'm quite happy with it. While working on a project like this, however, you always learn a few new things, lessons that you wish you had known at the beginning . . . and you always wish you had the chance to do just one more.

In this case, we got that chance. A few weeks after the release of the show, I was at a Random House sales conference in Fort Myers, Florida. People in the Audio department were very happy because we had gotten some pretty good press, including an exclusive story in a major newspaper, where the same space for an ad would have cost nearly twice what *Son of a Wanted Man*'s budget had been. If promoting the Random House Audio product line had been the goal, then we had already done very well. At lunch the executive in charge of the whole division, meaning Audio and several other departments, asked me what I wanted to do next. I almost didn't know what he was talking about. "Do another . . . ?" I couldn't believe my luck!

So, we got a chance to do one more, an audio drama version of "The Diamond of Jeru." And again we learned so much in the process that it was frustrating by the time we got to the end . . . but it was also a wonderful opportunity, and I'm eternally grateful because, as always with these audio dramas, I got to work with friends, and to make friends . . . and that has made producing them some of the best experiences in my life.

BEAU L'AMOUR
APRIL 2024

ABOUT LOUIS L'AMOUR

"I think of myself in the oral tradition—
as a troubadour, a village tale-teller,
the man in the shadows of the campfire.
That's the way I'd like to be remembered—
as a storyteller. A good storyteller."

IT IS DOUBTFUL that any author could be as at home in the world re-created in his novels as Louis Dearborn L'Amour. Not only could he physically fill the boots of the rugged characters he wrote about, but he literally "walked the land my characters walk." His personal experiences as well as his lifelong devotion to historical research combined to give Mr. L'Amour the unique knowledge and understanding of people, events, and the challenge of the American frontier that became the hallmarks of his popularity.

Of French-Irish descent, Mr. L'Amour could trace his own family in North America back to the early 1600s and follow their steady progression westward, "always on the frontier." As a boy growing up in Jamestown, North Dakota, he absorbed all he could about his family's frontier heritage, including the story of his great-grandfather who was scalped by Sioux warriors.

Spurred by an eager curiosity and desire to broaden his horizons, Mr. L'Amour left home at the age of fifteen and enjoyed a wide variety of jobs including seaman, lumberjack, elephant handler, skinner of dead cattle, miner, and an officer in the transportation corps during World War II. During his "yondering" days he also circled the world on a freighter, sailed a dhow on the Red Sea, was shipwrecked in the West Indies, and was stranded in the Mojave Desert. He won fifty-one of fifty-nine fights as a professional boxer and worked as a journalist and lecturer. He was a voracious reader and collector of books. His personal library contained 17,000 volumes.

Mr. L'Amour "wanted to write almost from the time I could talk." After developing a widespread following for his many frontier and adventure stories written for fiction magazines, Mr. L'Amour published his first full-length novel, *Hondo,* in the United States in 1953. Every one of his more than 120 books is in print; there are nearly 300 million copies of his books in print worldwide, making him one of the bestselling authors in modern literary history. His books have been translated into twenty languages, and more than forty-five of his novels and stories have been made into feature films and television movies.

His hardcover bestsellers include *The Lonesome Gods, The Walking Drum* (his twelfth-century historical novel), *Law of the Desert Born, Last of the Breed,* and *The Haunted Mesa.* His memoir, *Education of a Wandering Man,* was a leading bestseller in 1989. Audio dramatizations and adaptations of many L'Amour stories are available from Random House Audio Publishing.

The recipient of many great honors and awards, in 1983 Mr. L'Amour became the first novelist ever to be awarded the Congressional Gold Medal by the United States Congress in honor of his life's work. In 1984 he was also awarded the Medal of Freedom by President Reagan.

Louis L'Amour died on June 10, 1988. His wife, Kathy, and their two children, Beau and Angelique, carry the L'Amour publishing tradition forward.

louislamour.com

louislamourslosttreasures.com

louislamourgreatadventure.com